Stanislaus V. Henkels

The Valuable Collection of Autographs and Historical Papers

collected by the Hon. Jas. T. Mitchell of the Supreme Court of Penna. - also, The

entire Lincoln Memorial Collection of Chicago, Ill., at one time the personal

property of Abraham Lincoln

Stanislaus V. Henkels

The Valuable Collection of Autographs and Historical Papers
collected by the Hon. Jas. T. Mitchell of the Supreme Court of Penna. - also, The entire Lincoln Memorial Collection of Chicago, Ill., at one time the personal property of Abraham Lincoln

ISBN/EAN: 9783337392680

Printed in Europe, USA, Canada, Australia, Japan

Cover: Foto ©Andreas Hilbeck / pixelio.de

More available books at **www.hansebooks.com**

THE VALUABLE

Collection of Autographs

AND

HISTORICAL PAPERS

COLLECTED BY

THE HON. JAS. T. MITCHELL

OF THE SUPREME COURT OF PENNA.

—ALSO—

THE ENTIRE LINCOLN MEMORIAL COLLECTION

OF CHICAGO, ILL.

AT ONE TIME THE PERSONAL PROPERTY OF ABRAHAM LINCOLN

TO BE SOLD

Wednesday and Thursday, Dec. 5th and 6th, 1894

AFTERNOONS AND EVENINGS

COMMENCING AT 2 O'CLOCK AND 8 O'CLOCK

— .. ...

CATALOGUE COMPILED AND SALE
CONDUCTED BY
STAN. V. HENKELS

AT THE BOOK AUCTION ROOMS OF
THOS. BIRCH'S SONS
1110 Chestnut Street, Philada., Pa.

THE ONLY AUCTION HOUSE IN THE UNITED STATES WHERE AN EXPERT FILLS BOTH THE RÔLE OF CATALOGUER AND AUCTIONEER.

For those who cannot attend the sale, we take great pleasure in recommending the following gentlemen, who will accept orders for the sale:

JOSEPH F. SABIN,	80 Nassau street, New York.
S. B. LUYSTER,	79 Nassau street, New York.
J. S. BRADLEY, JR.,	Nassau and Liberty streets, New York.
W. E. BENJAMIN,	22 East Sixteenth street, New York.
W. R. BENJAMIN,	257 Fourth avenue, New York.
FRANCIS P. HARPER,	17 East Sixteenth street, New York.
DODD, MEAD & CO.,	Booksellers, New York.
C. L. TRAVER,	108 South Broad street, Trenton, N. J.
DAVID G. FRANCIS,	12 East Fifteenth street, New York.
GEO. E. LITTLEFIELD,	67 Cornhill, Boston, Massachusetts.
W. H. LOWDERMILK & CO.,	1424 F street, Washington, D.C.
ROBERT CLARKE & CO.,	61 W. Fourth street, Cincinnati, Ohio.
A. C. McCLURG & CO.,	117 Wabash avenue, Chicago, Ills.
CHAS. STEIGERWALT,	130 East King street, Lancaster.
W. H. CAMPION & CO.,	1001 Chestnut street, Philadelphia.
PORTER & COATES,	Chestnut and Juniper streets, Phila.
ED. FLOERCKEY,	Betz Building, Philadelphia.
GEO. H. RIGBY,	1123 Arch street, Philadelphia.
JOHN J. McVEY,	30 N. Thirteenth street, Philadelphia.
LEARY & CO.,	9 S. Ninth street, Philadelphia.

Or by the auctioneer, Stan. V. Henkels, 1110 Chestnut street, Philadelphia.

S. V. HENKELS, ESQ.

Dear Sir :—

I have concluded to send you all my Autographs, just as they are. I have been trying for a long while to get time to arrange them, but my portrait collection has reached such size and interest that it takes all the leisure I can command, and the Autographs will have to stand out of the way.

Yours truly,

JAMES T. MITCHELL.

August 24, 1894.

REMARKS.

THIS valuable accumulation of autograph letters and his-torical documents is the outcome of many years of untiring research by the Hon. James T. Mitchell, it being his intention to make up a complete set of all the Colonial and recent American Judges; but as his main hobby has always been the collecting of rare engraved portraits, and as his duties as a Justice of the Supreme Court of Pennsylvania have proved so arduous—taking up most all of his time—he has found it necessary, in order to make one collection complete, to give up one or the other—either the autographs or the portraits. He has decided, therefore, to follow the bent of his feelings and continue collecting portraits, and consequently has placed the collection of autographs in my hands to be sold.

It is one of the very few opportunities that have been offered for years to possess fine specimens of autographs of prominent characters of the American revolutionary period; of the early Puritans, who had to do with the witches and witchcraft; of rare names connected with the judicial history of our country; of persons who have obtained prominence in the literary world; of American military heroes, etc. In fact, there is not a page in the whole catalogue but what contains some one item of interest. Judge Mitchell's letter, which heads this short preamble, explains his reason for selling.

LINCOLN MEMORIAL COLLECTION.

The material enumerated in the catalogue, under the above heading, embraces the entire collection of the Lincoln Memorial Association, which was viewed by hundreds of thousands of Lincoln's admirers while on exhibition in Chicago; and it was admitted that it contained more items of interest relating to the great and good man than any other collection of the kind in the country. It embraces the furniture from Lincoln's house, purchased at the time he left Springfield to take his seat at Washington as President; also his marriage certificate, legal papers, letters, documents, law-books, etc., each fully authenticated by direct purchasers from Abraham Lincoln.

There are also several relics at the end of the catalogue that should attract the attention of those interested in relics of the Plymouth Pilgrims.

STAN. V. HENKELS.

CATALOGUE.

JUSTICES OF THE SUPREME COURT OF THE UNITED STATES.

1 BALDWIN, HENRY. 1822–1844. A. L. S. 4to. 3 pp. Pittsburg, Feb. 19, 1826.

2 Baldwin, Henry. A. L. S. 4to. 4 pp. Oct. 17, 1825.

3 Barbour, Philip P. 1836–1841. A. L. S. 4to. Washington, Jan. 16, 1823.

4 Blair, John. 1789–1796. Signer of the Constitution. A. L. S. 4to. Williamsburg, Oct. 6, 1782.

   Fine specimen. Interceding for a British prisoner captured with Lord Cornwallis, at Yorktown.

5 Blatchford, Saml. A. L. S. 8vo. New York, Dec. 18, 1868.

6 Bradley, Jos. P. 1870. A. L S. 4to. Washington, April 8, 1870.

7 Bradley, Jos. P. A. L. S. 8vo. Washington, Jan. 21, 1882.

8 CAMPBELL, JOHN A. 1853–1861. A. L. S. 4to. Mobile, Feb. 24, 1845.

9 Catron, John. 1837–1865. A. L. S. 4to. March 12, 1839.

10 Catron, John. A. L. S. (With initials). 4to. No date.

11 Chase, Salmon P. Chief Justice. 1864–1873. A. L. S. 4to. 2 pp. Baltimore, Oct. 16, 1831.

12 Chase, Saml. 1796–1811. Signer of the Declaration of Independence. A. D. S. Small 4to, inlaid. Baltimore, April 1, 1809.

13 Clifford, Nathan. 1858. A. L. S. 8vo. 2 pp. Washington, Feb. 18, 1871.

14 Curtis, Benj. R. 1851–1857. A. L. S. 4to. Pittsfield, Oct. 29, 1853.

15 Curtis, Benj. R. A. L. S. 8vo. 2 pp. Boston, April 13, 1869.

16 Cushing, Wm. (Appointed Chief Justice, but declined). 1789–1810. A. L. S. 4to. Boston, July 2, 1807.

17 Cushing, Wm. A. L. S. 4to. 2 pp. Scituate, July 3, 1794.

18 DANIEL, PETER V. 1841–1860. A. L. S. 4to. 2 pp. Richmond, July 7, 1828.

19 Daniel, Peter V. A. L. S. 4to. Richmond, Jan. 3, 1835.

20 Davis, David. 1862–1877. A. L. S. 8vo. 2 pp. Bloomington, Aug. 3, 1864.

21 Duval, Gabriel. 1811–1836. A. L. S. 4to. 2 pp. Marietta, Oct. 30, 1828.

22 Duval, Gabriel. A. L. S. 4to. 2 pp. Washington, Aug. 23, 1808.

23 ELLSWORTH, OLIVER, Chief Justice. 1796. A. L. S. 4to. April 20. No year.

24 Ellsworth, Oliver. Two A. D's. S. Small 4tos.

25 FIELD, STEPHEN J. 1863. A. L. S. 4to. Washington, March 6, 1865.

26 Fuller, Melville W. A. L. S. 4to. Chicago, March 7, 1871.

27 GRAY, HORACE. A. L. S. 8vo. Washington, Nov. 5, 1888.

28 Grier, Robert C. 1846–1870. A. L. S. 4to. Pittsburg, Nov. 18, 1854.

29 HARLAN, JOHN M. 1877. A. L. S. 8vo. Washington, May 23, 1881.

30 Harrison, Robt. H. 1789–1790. Aide to General Washington. A. L. S. Folio. June 1, 1780. To Col. Dayton. With address.

31 IREDELL, JAMES. 1790–1799. A. L. S. 4to. 2 pp. Richmond, June 7, 1793.

32 Iredell, James. A. L. S. 4to, inlaid. Edenton, N. C., Oct. 27, 1795.

33 JAY, JOHN, Chief Justice. 1789–1791. President of the Continental Congress. A. L. S. 4to. 2 pp. Albany, Sept. 4, 1798.

34 Jay, John. A. L. S. 4to. Phildadelphia, Jan. 6, 1779.

35 Johnson, Thos. 1791–1793. Member of the Continental Congress. A. L. S. 4to. Annapolis, Jan. 11, 1778. To Elias Boudinot. With address.

36 Johnson, Wm. 1804–1834. A. L. S. 4to. 2 pp. Charleston, May 30, 1827. With address.

37 Johnson, Wm. A. L. S. 4to. 3 pp. Charleston, May 27, 1822. With address.

38 LAMAR, L. Q. C. A. L. S. 4to. Washingtoh, May 13, 1858.

39 Lamar, L. Q. C. A. L. S. 4to. Oxford, Miss. Aug. 14, 1868.

40 Livingston, Brockholst. 1806-1823. A. L. S. Folio. New York, April 15, 1786. With address.

41 Livingston, Brockholst. A. L. S. Folio. New York, Aug. 19, 1801. With address.

42 McKINLEY, JOHN. 1837-1852. A. L. S. 4to. 2 pp. Louisville, Dec. 22, 1842. With address.

43 McKinley, Jno. A. L. S. 4to. 2 pp. Washington, April 20, 1828.

44 McLean, John. 1829-1861. A. L. S. 4to. Washington, Dec. 14, 1826.

45 Marshall, John. Chief Justice. 1801-1835. Wrote the Life of Washington. A. L. S. 4to. Mount Vernon, Sep. 5, 1798. With address.

46 Matthews, Stanley. A. L. S. 4to. Cincinnati, Dec. 20, 1865.

47 Miller, Saml. F. 1862. A. L. S. 4to. 3 pp. Keokuk, Nov. 18, 1867.

48 Miller, Saml. F. Autograph Legal Opinion, as Supreme Court Judge. 13 pp. Folio. 1867.

49 Moore, Alfred. 1779-1804. A. L. S. 4to. 2 pp. Colonel Read's, Dec. 17, 1795. To Jno. f. Grimké. With address.

> Choice specimen and very rare.

50 NELSON, SAML. 1845-1872. A. L. S. Folio. 2 pp. Cooperstown, Sep. 23, 1830.

51 Nelson, Saml. A. L. S. 8vo. 3 pp. Feb. 5. (No year).

52 PATERSON, WM. 1793-1806. Member of the Old Congress and Governor of New Jersey. A. L. S. 4to. 4 pp. New Brunswick, Feb. 8, 1801.

53 Paterson, Wm. D. S. Folio. New Brunswick, Dec. 18, 1792. With seal.

54 RUTLEDGE, JOHN. 1789-1791, Member of the Old Congress and Governor of South Carolina. A. L. S. 4to. May 22, 1795. With address.

55 Rutledge, John. A. L. S. 4to. 3 pp. Cambridge, Nov. 21, 1793.

56 Rutledge, John. A. L. S. 4to. No place, no date.

4

57 STANTON, EDWIN M. 1869. A. L. S. 4to. Washington, Jan. 26, 1863.

58 Story, Joseph. 1811–1845. A. L. S. 4to. 2 pp. Salem, Dec. 1, 1826.

59 Story, Joseph. A. L. S. 4to. 3 pp. Washington, March 21, 1825. With address.

60 Swayne, Noah H. 1862. A. L. S. 8vo. Washington, Dec. 4, 1868.

16 TANEY, ROGER B. Chief Justice. 1836–1864. A. L. S. 4to. Aug. 25, 1824.

62 Taney, Roger B. A. L. S. 4to. Baltimore, Nov. 6, 1854.

63 Thompson, Smith. 1823–1843. A. L. S. 4to. 3 pp. Poughkeepsie, July 30, 1828. With address.

64 Thompson, Smith. A. L. S. 4to. 3 pp. Aug. 26, 1823.

65 Todd, Thos. 1807–1826. A. L. S. 4to. 2 pp. Frankfort, July 9, 1802. With address.

66 Trimble, Robert. 1826–1828. A. L. S. 4to. 3 pp. Bourbon Co., Jan. 30, 1819.

67 WAITE, MORRISON R. Chief Justice. 1874. A. L. S. 8vo. 2 pp. Washington, April 17, 1882.

68 Washington, Bushrod. 1798–1829. Executor of Gen. Washington's Estate. A. L. S. 4to. Philadelphia, Oct. 8, 1818. With address.

69 Washington, Bushrod. A. L. S. 4to. 2 pp. Richmond, May 17, 1797.

70 Wayne, James M. 1835–1867. A. L. S. 4to. 2 pp. West Point, March, 11, 1850.

71 Wayne, James M. A. L. S. 4to. 3 pp. Savannah, May, 1836. With address.

72 Wilson, James. 1789–1798. Signer of the Declaration of Independence. A. L. S. 4to. Aug. 22, 1791. With address.

73 Woodbury, Levi. 1845–1872. A. L. S. 4to. Washington, Aug. 14, 1841. With address.

74 Woodbury, Levi. A. L. S. 4to. Washington, Sept. 11, 1837.

Newport ye 31 March 1787

Sir/

    I have Recepted to John
Sayles Esq for Eighty three & one third
Dollars and there is no noccation of our
paſing Recepts you will pleaſe to give
Direction for me to Draw in No York 33⅓
Dollars informing there is so much Due
to me which with the 50 I have Recd
will make 83⅓ and the Remainder to make
one Hundred being 16⅔ two thirds I will
Recpt to you for on the terms we agreed
Pleaſe to Send pr firſt Conveyance

    I am Sir your Aſſured
Freiend & Servt

        Peleg Arnold

No. 76

MEMBERS OF THE CONTINENTAL CONGRESS.

75 ADAMS, ANDREW, from Connecticut. Chief Justice of that State. A. L. S. Folio. Litchfield, April 1, 1772.

76 Arnold, Peleg, from Rhode Island. Chief Justice of that State. A. L. S. 4to. Newport, March 31, 1787.
Rare.

77 Arnold, Peleg. A. L. S. 4to. Smithfield, March 25, 1777. With address.
Rare.

78 BANISTER, JOHN, from Virginia. One of the framers of the Articles of Confederation, Colonel in the Virginia Line. A. L. S. Folio. 2 pp. Jan. 1, 1772. With address.
Rare.

79 Banister, John. A. L. S. 4to. Jan. 14, 1786.
Rare.

80 Bayard, John, from Pennsylvania. Commanded the Second Battalion of Philadelphia at the Battle of Trenton. A. L. S. 4to. Philadelphia, Jan, 12, 1787. To his daughter. With address.

81 Bedford, Gunning, from Delaware ; of which State he was Governor. Officer in the Revolution. A. L. S. Small 4to. Jan. 29, 178-.
Requesting the Librarian of the Philadelphia Library that his son be allowed to take out books on his account.

82 Bee, Thomas, from South Carolina. 2 A. D's. S. Small 4to. (Checks). Charleston, Jan. 1, 1797, and July 2, 1798.
One contains an embossed impression of a United States twenty-five-cent revenue stamp.

83 Benson, Egbert, from New York. Was one of the three commissioners to direct the embarkation of the Tory refugees in 1783. A. L. S. Folio. Poughkeepsie, July 11, 1788. With address.

84 Benson, Egbert. A. L. S. 4to. April 1, 1801. To Gov. John Jay.
"I am to inform your Excellency that having been appointed, I have this day accepted the office of a Circuit Judge of the United States."

85 Bland, Theodorick, from Virginia. Captain of the First Troop of Virginia Cavalry, in the Revolution. Chancellor of Virginia. L. S. 4to. 3 pp. June, 1781.

    This in the handwriting of and signed by Joseph Jones, member of the Old Congress, from Virginia. The contents are very interesting, relating to news of the arrival of the French fleet and of General Wayne's movements.

86 Boudinot, Elias, from New Jersey. Commissary General of Prisoners in the Revolution. A. L. S. Folio. Rosehill, near Philadelphia, Nov. 11, 1802.

87 Boudinot, Elias. A. D. S. 4to. April, 1785.

88 Boudinot, Elias. D. S. 4to. Dec. 24, 1817.

89 Bradford, William, from Rhode Island, (but never took his seat). President of the United States Senate, *pro tem.* A. L. S. 4to. Rohoboth, Jan. 8, 1779. To Colonel Jackson. With address.

    Written while practicing medicine. A masterpiece of spelling. Rare.

90 Brownson, Nathan, from Georgia. Of which State he was Governor. A. L. S. 4to. Oct. 29, 1755. With address.

91 Brownson, Nathan. D. S. Folio. Nov. 6, 1776.

92 CHASE, JEREMIAH TOWNLEY, from Maryland. Justice of the Court of Appeals. A. L. S. 4to. Annapolis, May 20, 1782. With address.

93 Clay, Joseph, from Georgia. Justice of the United States District Court. A. L. S. 4to. 4 pp. Savannah, July 31, 1797. To General Jackson.

94 Clay, Joseph. D. S. Folio. Savannah, Jan. 9, 1780.

95 Carroll, Daniel, from Maryland. D. S. 4to. N. P., N. D.

    Signed also by Thomas Johnson, member of the Continental Congress from Maryland, and Brigadier-General in the Revolution.

    A receipt for a lot of ground in the city of Washington. Signed by all three of the commissioners—Thomas Johnson, David Stuart and Daniel Carroll.

96 DANA, FRANCIS, from Massachusetts. Delegate to the Constitutional Convention. Justice of the Supreme Court of Massachusetts. D. S. 4to. Dec. 6, 1797.

97 Dickinson, Philemon, from New Jersey. Commanded the New Jersey Militia at the Battle of Monmouth. A. L. S. 8vo. Hermitage, Aug. 16, 1807. With address.

98 Duane, James, from New York. Signer of the Articles of Confederation ; first Mayor of New York city. A. L. S. 4to. 2 pp. (1790).

99 Duane, James. A. L. S. Folio. New York, Aug. 9, 1773.

Rehoboth January 8th ad 1779

Dear Sir.

I am now at the house of Mr Jesse
Sanders. he informs me that he is a
Soldier under your command. and that he
is ordered to joyne the regement and
has requested me to informe you of his
persent State of health. he is now
very much unwell with a Rumatitch
Disorder confined to his house. and has
bin under a corse of medicines for the same
from me, for sum time: and at this Time
is impossable for him to attend his Duty
as a Solder. And am Dr Sr with
Every Sentiment of Esteem your most
obediant and Humbl Servent

William Bradford

To Conll Jackson

No. 89.

Middletown May 9th 1775 —

Sir

I have seen as many of the Com: as I could conveniently and we have agreed to nominate as a Post Master for this Town Mr. Wensley Hobby, a Gentleman of acknowledged Ability and Integrity, and known attachment to the American cause, and one that possesses in a high Degree the Confidence of the People of this Town. I am Sir

your obed. & hum. Servant.

Titus Hosmer

W. G. —

No. 112.

100 Duane, James. A. L. S. Folio. July 22, 1780. To Governor Clinton.

Asking for information respecting the French fleet.

101 Duane, James. D. S. As Mayor of New York. Folio. April 7, 1787. With fine impressions of the seal.

102 EDWARDS, PIERPONT, from Connecticut. Served in the Revolutionary Army. Justice of the United States District Court and of the Superior Court of Connecticut. A. L. S. 4to. New York, June 23, 1788. With address.

103 Edwards, Pierpont. A. L. S. 4to. New York, Feb. 21, 1786. To Hon. Jonathan Dayton. With address.

104 FEW, WM., from Georgia. Colonel in the Revolution. L. S. 4to. New York, March 29, 1814.

105 GRIFFIN, CYRUS, from Virginia. President of the Continental Congress. Justice of the Supreme Court. Chancellor of the Virginia United States District Court. A. L. S. 4to. Williamsburg, Aug. 4, 1805.

105 HARTLEY, THOMAS, from Pennsylvania. Colonel in the Revolution. A. L. S. 4to. Yorktown, Sep. 6, 1796.

107 Hemsley, Wm., from Maryland. A. L. S. 4to. Queen Ann's County, Dec. 26, 1799. With address.

108 Higginson, Stephen, from Massachusetts. Aided in putting down Shay's Rebellion. A. L. S. 4to. 2 pp. Boston, Oct. 8, 1791. With address.

109 Higginson, Stephen. A. L. S. 4to. 2 pp. Boston, March 20, 1792.

110 Hillhouse, James, from Connecticut. A. L. S. 4to. 6 pp. Philada., March 2, 1793. To Gov. Huntington.

A very interesting letter, in which he narrates the proceedings for the impeachment of the Secretary of the Treasury (Alex. Hamilton), for a violation of his duty, and his honorable acquittal by a great majority of the House.

111 Hillhouse, James. A. L. S. Folio. New Haven, Oct. 2, 1792. To Saml. Huntington. With address.

Acknowledging the receipt of his commission to serve in the Congress of the United States.

112 Hosmer, Titus, from Connecticut. Justice of the Court of Appeals. A. L. S. Oblong 4to. Middletown, May 7, 1775. To Wm. Goddard. With address.

"I have seen as many of the Com'tee as I could conveniently, and we have agreed to nominate as a Postmaster for this Town Mr. Wensley Hobby, a Gentleman of Acknowledged Ability and Integrity, and known attachment to the American cause, and one that possesses in a high Degree the Confidence of the people of the Town."

Rare.

8

113 Hosmer, Titus. _ Autograph Memoranda Book ; being the
"Dockett, Hartford County Court, April 2, Tuesday,
Anno Domini, 1773." 22 pp. 8vo.

114 Houstoun, John, from Georgia, and Governor of that State.
A. L. S. 4to. 2 pp. Savannah, Oct. 9, 1784. With
address.

115 Houstoun, John. A. L. S. 4to. 2 pp. Cathead, Feb. 11,
1788. With address.

116 Howell, David, from Rhode Island. Justice of the Supreme
Court. A. L. S. 4to. Providence, July 31, 1797. With
address.

117 Howell, David. A. L. S. 4to. 3 pp. Providence, Sep.
24, 1798.

118 Huntington, Benjamin, from Connecticut. A. L. S. Folio.
2 pp. Philada., Dec. 28, 1790. With address.

119 Huntington, Benjamin. A. L. S. 4to. Norwich, Nov. 10,
1770. To Capt. Jabez Huntington. With address.

120 JOHNSON, THOMAS, from Maryland. Nominated
Washington to be Commander-in-chief. Brig.-Gen.
in the Revolution. Justice of the Supreme Court of
the United States. A. L. S. 4to. Frederick, Oct.
30, 1809.

121 Johnston, Samuel, from North Carolina. Governor of that
State. A. L. S. · 4to. 3 pp. Hayes, June 7, 1787.

122 Johnston, Samuel. D. S. Folio. March 13, 1793.
Signed also by Clement Biddle, colonel in the Revolutionary War.

123 Jones, Joseph, from Virginia. Friend and political confidant
of Gen. Washington. A. L. S. Folio. 3 pp. Jan. 2,
1781. To Theodorick Bland. With address.
Interesting letter, relative to what stand France and Spain would
take in reference to the American colonies.

124 KINSEY, JAMES, from New Jersey, and Chief Justice
of that State. A. L. S. 4to. 2 pp. July 2, 1779.

125 Kinsey, James. A. L. S. 4to. Dec. 22, 1786.

126 LANSING, JOHN, from New York. Member of the
Constitutional Convention. Chief Justice and Chancellor. A. L. S. 4to. Jan. 17, 1818. With address.

127 Lansing, John. Part of A. L. S. 7 pp. To Gov. Jay.
Report, as Chief Justice, on the case of Benj. Holmes, convicted, in
Washington, of murder, July 8, 1799.

128 Law, Richard, from Connecticut. Appointed by Washington U. S. District Judge. A. D. S. 4to. March 31, 1800.

129 Law, Richard. D. S. Folio. Sep. 25, 1788.

130 Laurance, John, from New York. Colonel in the Revolutionary War. Conducted the trial of Major John André. Justice of the United States District Court. A. L. S. 4to. New York, July 24, 1809. To Garrett Van Schaack. With address.

131 Laurance, John. A. L. S. Folio. New York, April 20, 1807. To Garrett Van Schaack. With address.

132 Livermore, Samuel, from New Hampshire. President *pro tem.* of the U. S. Senate. A. L. S. Folio. Exeter, Sep. 27, 1785.

133 Livermore, Saml. A. D. S. 4to. Middlesex, Oct. 1, 1771.

134 Livingston, Robert R., from New York. Chancellor of New York. Administered the oath of office to Washington upon his inauguration as President. Friend and partner of Fulton. A. L. S. Folio. 3 pp. New York, May 22, 1812. To Peter Du Ponceau. With address.
Very interesting letter relative to the times (War of 1812).

135 Livingston, Robt. R. A. L. S. 4to. Nov. 12, 1807.

136 Lovell, James, from Massachusetts. Imprisoned by Gage after the Battle of Bunker Hill. Autograph on franked address. Small 4to.

137 Lowell, John, from Massachusetts. One of "Midnight Judges in 1801." A. L. S. 4to. Roxbury, April 13, 1799. With address.

138 Lowell, John. A. L. S. 4to. 3 pp. Boston, Oct. 8, 1796. With address.

139 MARCHANT, HENRY, from Rhode Island. Signer of the Articles of Confederation. Justice of the Supreme Court. A. L. S. 4to. 3 pp. Newport, Oct. 18, 1788.

140 Marchant, Henry. A. L. S. 4to. 3 pp. New York, July 12, 1787.

141 Marchant, Henry. A. D. S. Folio. New York, July 10, 1792.

142 Martin, Luther, from Maryland. Member of the Annapolis Convention. A. L. S. Folio. Baltimore, Sept. 10, 1791.

143 Matlack, Timothy, from Pennsylvania. Officer in the Revolution. 2 D. S's. 4to and folio. 1817.

143½ Mercer, James, from Virginia. L. S. 4to. Dumfries, May 15, 1789.
    The letter written and also signed by Richard Parker.

144 Mitchell, Stephen Mix, from Connecticut. Chief Justice of that State. A. L. S. Folio. Jan. 5, 1807.

145 Mitchell, Stephen Mix. A. L. S. Folio. 3 pp. New Town, Feb. 5, 1770. With address.

146 NASH, ABNER, from North Carolina; of which State he was Governor. A. D. S. 4to. Oct. 9, 1778.
    Signed also by General Griffith Rutherford of the Revolutionary War.

147 OTIS, SAML. A., from Massachusetts. L. S. 4to. 1797.

148 Otis, Saml. A. L. S. April 2, 1801.

149 PENDLETON, EDMUND, from Virginia. A. L. S. 4to. Nov. 1, 1764. With address.

150 Peters, Richard, from Pennsylvania. A. L. S. 4to. 2 pp. Belmont, Aug. 31, 1788. To Baron Steuben. With address.
    Highly eulogistic of General Steuben, and lamenting that Congress had not acted in his case.

151 Peters, Richard. A. L. S. Folio. War Office, July 17, 1781. To Capt. David Hopkins. With address.
    In reference to Captain Hopkins's promotion in the ranks, together with a copy of a letter from the "Board of War" to General Washington, May 1, 1781.

152 Pettit, Chas., from Pennsylvania. A. L. S. 4to. Burlington, Jan. 13, 1772. With address.

153 Pettit, Chas. A. L. S. 4to. Philadelphia, May 18, 1792. With address.

154 Plater, George, from Maryland, and Governor of that State. L. S. Folio. June 22, 1766.

155 Potts, Richard, from Maryland. A. L. S. 4to. Fredericktown, Jan. 17, 1791.

156 READ, JACOB, from South Carolina. Officer in the Revolution. Justice of the United States District Court. A. L. S. 4to. Charlestown, April 17, 1799. With address.

157 Read, Jacob. Part of D. S. 4to. Signed by Isaac Huger.

158 Ridgely, Richard, from Maryland. A. L. S. Folio. Dec. 15, 1785.

Philadelphia Sept 8th 1779

Dear Sir

Yours of the 22nd ult: came duly to hand
I most heartily regret the Misfortune of our fleet
at Penobscot — 'tis the fortune of war — Spain
has at length taken an active part in the war
with France against England — 'tis believed
that England will make further overtures of peace
to America but all will be of no avail untill
She acknowledges our Independance — a brig
has arrived from St Eustatia with 40 Tun of powder —
Congress has resolved that they will on no account
whatever emit more than 200,000,000 of dollars
& mean to depend on the Exertions of the States by
loans & Taxes to Supply the Treasury —

I send herewith a paper to which I refer you for
the News — the Journals you mention are to be
had — the difficulty lies in the Conveyance my compliments
to mrs Ellsworth —

I am dear Sir with respect & esteem
your Obedt humble Servt

Oliver Ellsworth Esqr   Jesse Root

turn over

PS: mr Drayton was buried last
Saturday he died of a putrid nervous fever

No. 161.

159   Rodney, Thomas, from Delaware. A. L. S. 4to. Washington, Dec. 15, 1804. With address.

160   Rodney, Thos. A. L. S. 4to. Duck Creek, Oct. 10, 1801.

161   Root, Jesse, from Connecticut. Colonel in the Revolution. Justice of the Supreme Court of Connecticut. A. L. S. 4to. Philadelphia, Sept. 8, 1779. To Oliver Ellsworth.
Fine specimen. Rare.

> "I most heartily regret the misfortune of our fleet at Penobscot—it is the fortune of war. Spain has at length taken an active part in the war with France against England—it's believed that England will make further overtures of peace to America, but all will be of no avail untill she acknowledges our Independence."

162   Root, Jesse. A. L. S. 4to. Windham, March 14, 1798. With address.

163   Rumsey, Benjamin, from Maryland. A. L. S. Folio. 2 pp. Charles Town, Sep. 10, 1768.

164   Rutledge, John, from South Carolina, and Governor of that State. Appointed Chief Justice of the U. S., by Washington, but not confirmed. Autograph draft of a letter to the President of the United States (George Washington). Folio. 3 pp. May 13, 1791.

> * * * "but summoned again, as you were, from your retirement by the united voice and the obvious wellfare of your country, you did not hesitate to furnish one more Proof that, in comparision to the great Duties of social life, all objects of a private Nature are with you but secondary considerations, and to this your ruling Passion of Love for your country it is that we owe the opportunity now offered of congratulating you on your safe arrival in the city of Savannah. An office, we the committee, under the strongest impressions of sensibility and attachment, execute in the name and Behalf of a respected and grateful number of Citizens.
>
> "History furnishes Instances of some eminently qualified for the field, and of others endowed with Talents adequate to the intricate affairs of state, but you, sir, have enriched the Annals of America with a proof to be sent abroad to all mankind that however rare the association, the Virtues and Talents of Soldier and republican statesman will sometimes dwell together and both characters derive additional lustre from a subserviency to the Precepts of Religion," etc.

165   SCOTT, GUSTAVUS, from Maryland. A. L. S. 4to. Washington, Sept. 20, 1796. With address.

166   Sedgwick, Theodore, from Massachusetts. Served in the Revolutionary Expedition to Canada, in 1776. A. L. S. Folio. 4 pp. Stockbridge, Nov. 19, 1796.

167   Sedgwick, Theodore. Autograph Opinion. 20 pp. Folio.
Opinion in the case of the canvassers of votes, Clinton and Jay's election, Aug., 1792.

168 Sergeant, Jonathan Dickinson, from New Jersey. Attorney-
General of Pennsylvania.   A. L. S.   Folio.   2 pp.
Princeton, April 24, 1775.   To the Committee of In-
spection and Correspondence, at Elizabethtown.

Highly important letter voicing the sentiments of the New Jersey
patriots.

" To the Committee of Correspondence for the Borough of Elizabeth.

"GENTLEMEN:—The very alarming Intelligence we have just received induces us to fear that the Friends of American Liberty will be
compelled to resort to the last Appeal for the Protection of their Rights.
In this Extremity when no Time should be lost from Preparation, we
think that a Communication of Sentiment from the different Parts of
our Province should take Place, and that no Mode of doing this is so
proper as that of a Provincial Congress. Should our Brethren concur
with us in this Opinion, we would be glad that the Members of the
Committee of Correspondence for the Province, to whom it seems to
belong, would, together with the Chairman, appoint a speedy Day for
such Convention. These Sentiments, should they even appear to be
erroneous, will need no Apology as they come from Persons who would
wish not to be wanting to the common Cause; and the Suddenness of
the Occasion hardly admits of formally convening the different Committees. Several of the Committee of Correspondence are in your Neighborhood, or within your Influence, which is the Reason of our address-
ing ourselves to you in this Way.

"The above is taken as the Sense of a Meeting of the Inhabitants of
Princeton and the Neighborhood, together with some of the Members of
the Committees of Somerset, Middlesex and Hunterdon.—It is further
desired of our Brethren to consider whether it may not be proper to fix
some Day shortly before the Meeting of the Continental Congress and
not too early to be notified to the more distant Parts of the Colony.—
We have thought of Friday, 5 May.

"By order of the Meeting,

"Dated at Princeton,   JONA D. SERGEANT, Clerk.
"24 April, 1775.

"P. S.—It is requested the Contents of this Letter may be communi-
cated on the Passage to the Committees at N. Brunswick & Woodbridge."

169 Sergeant, Jonathan D. A. D. S. Folio.   April 29, 1774.

170 Sergeant, Jonathan D. A. L. S. Folio. Philada.,·May 4,
1792. To Col. Aaron Burr. With address.

171 Sitgreaves, John, from North Carolina. Aide-de-camp to
Gov. Caswell at the Battle of Camden. A. L. S. 4to.
Halifax, April 1, 1798.

172 Smith, Jonathan B., from Pennsylvania. Signer of the
Articles of Confederation. Judge of the Common Pleas
of Philadelphia. A. L. S. Small 4to. Jan. 27, 1779.

173 Smith, Jonathan B. A. D. S. 4to. Philada., 1785.

174 Smith, Melancton, from New York. A. D. S. Folio.
3 pp. Jan. 18, 1791.

175   Smith, Melancton.   D. S. (twice).   4to.   January 24, 1779.

177   Sullivan, James, from Massachusetts, and Governor of that State. A. L. S. Folio. June 24, 1807. To John Hawthorn. With address.

178   Sullivan, James. A. L. S. Folio. Boston, July 25, 1807.

179   Sullivan, John, from New Hampshire. Major-General in the Revolutionary War. A. D. S. Folio. 1785.

180   Symmes, John Cleves, from New Jersey. Served in the Revolutionary Army, and distinguished himself in covering the retreat of Gen. Washington. Justice of the Supreme Court of New Jersey. A. L. S. (in the third person). Folio. Feb. 3, 1797. To Elias Boudinot, Jr.

    A caustic letter to Mr. Boudinot, in answer to accusations relative to the "Miami Purchase."

181   Symmes, John Cleves. A. L. S. Folio. 4to. 3 pp. Cincinnati, Aug. 5, 1804. To Jonathan Dayton. With address.

182   Symmes, John Cleves. A. L. S. Folio. 6 pp. Northbend, May 21, 1790. To Elias Boudinot. With address.

    Very interesting letter, narrating the depredations by the Indians and the uselessness of trying to convert them.

183   TREADWELL, JOHN, from Connecticut. Governor of that State. A. L. S. 4to. Farmington, Sept. 5, 1809.

184   Treadwell, John. A. D. S. Folio. June 24, 1782.

185   Tucker, Thos. T., from South Carolina. L. S. 4to. Washington, May 24, 1824.

186   VAN DYKE, NICHOLAS, from Delaware. Signer of the Articles of Confederation. Chief Justice of Delaware. A. D. S. Folio. July 8, 1825.

187   WADSWORTH, JEREMIAH, from Connecticut. Justice of Court of Appeals. A. L. S. 4to. Hartford, June 22, 1799.

188   Wadsworth, Jeremiah. A. L. S. 4to. No place, no date. With address.

189   Wentworth, Jno., from New Hampshire. D. S. 4to. Jan. 8, 1775. With seal of New Hampshire.

190 Wingate, Paine, from New Hampshire. A. L. S. 4to.
     Phila., Dec. 8, 1791. To Christ Tappan. With address.

> "I have this evening received the disagreeable news of the defeat of
> General St. Clair. We have not an official account, but there are letters
> in this city which came in such way and with such particular circum-
> stances as to leave little or no doubt, in the opinion of any one I have
> seen, of the melancholy fact. The imformation is that on Nov. 4, Gen-
> eral St. Clair had approached within about fifteen miles of the Miami
> towns with twelve hundred Continental militia troops; that he was ap-
> prised of the Indians hovering around him & expected an attack & had
> disposed his men to recieve them. That the Indians made their assault
> about day-light in the morning by firing once & then immediately rush-
> ing on to our men with their other weapons of death. That their prin-
> cipal attack was aimed against that part of our army where the militia
> were posted, who soon gave way & a sad slaughter ensued. It is said
> that we have lost six hundred men, among whom there are between
> thirty and forty officers." Etc.

191 Wolcott, Erastus, from Connecticut. Brig.-Gen. in the
     Revolution. A. D. S. 4to. New Haven, Oct. 30, 1772.
     Rare.

192 YATES, PETER W., from New York. A. L. S. 4to.
     Albany, Jan. 12, 1785. With address.

> "Yesterday it was resolved to have a Procession in this city next St.
> John's day, the 24 inst., when you will be pleased to favor us with
> your company and to invite also such worthy Brethren as reside in your
> neighbourhood to come and join in the Procession."

193 Yates, Robt. W. A. L. S. 4to. July 3, 1815. With ad-
     dress.

194 Yates, Robt. W. A. L. S. 4to. 2 pp. Aug. 20, 1818.
     With address.

SIGNERS OF THE DECLARATION OF INDEPENDENCE.

195   **A**DAMS, JOHN. Second President of the United States. Parchment D. S. Folio. Dec. 20, 1798. With seal.

> The commission of Bushrod Washington, appointing him one of the Justices of the Supreme Court of the United States.

196   **B**ARTLETT, JOSIAH. A. L. S. 4to. Kingston, Jan. 19, 1789.

> Fine specimen.

197   **E**LLERY, WM. A. L. S. 4to. Sept. 24; 1781.

> Fine specimen.

198   **G**ERRY, ELBRIDGE. A. L. S. Folio. 4 pp. Phila., Sep. 6, 1776. To John Wendell. With address.

> Highly important historical letter, written in the year of the signing of the Declaration of Independence.
>
> "Our affairs in Canada wear a favorable Appearance, or rather at Ticonderoga & Crown Point; where by ye last returns ye Army were ab't thirteen thousand strong of w'ch about 3000 were unfit for Duty, in addition to these six other Regiments were on their March from Connecticut & Massachusetts, & about four Regiments at other different posts, at New York things for ye present are a little shattered by Means of ye Retreat, but ye Skirmish on long Island has served to convince our Army that they are now able with ye Regiments that are disciplined, to meet ye Enemy on equal Terms. General Lee is ordered to reinforce them with several Regiments from ye Southward & one from Rhode Island & with firm Conduct our Generals may yet baffle ye Enemy. There is reason to imagine that ye Enemy have suffered more than our Army including ye captives, & Lord Howe has sent to Congress by General Sullivan a Desire of conferring w'th some Members of its Body in a private Capacity, not doubting that he can afford such Terms of peace as will be acceptable & proposing to treat w'th ye Congress when ye same are acceded to, but the whole is considered as an artifice to divide, by leading ye people to suppose that his Lordship has used every Method for obtaining Peace while on our Part they have been rejected. to turn ye Stratagem upon him Congress have resolved that being ye Representatives of ye independent States of America, they cannot send a Committee but in their public Capacity, & that being ever ready to listen to Terms of peace they will send a Committee to know his Lordship's Powers & proposals & to enquire what ye Terms are which he has to offer to ye Continent. The Committee are appointed, altho' against ye Mind of every Member from ye State which I represent, as well as Rhode Island & Georgia who are apprehensive that ye Appointment previous to his Lordship's assurance that he will receive them will wear ye Appearance of an over great Desire for Peace which is neither consistent with Dignity or true Policy & be construed as an Act of Timidity very discouraging to ye States & animating to ye Enemy, but ye Gentlemen on ye other Side are very desirous of drawing out his Lordship's proposals that if good they may be accepted & if bad exposed, which is a good Design if accomplished in a way that will not disagreebly effect ye Continent. It is expected that ye Committee will not be received, & if they are, any proposals w'ch his Lordship may offer that do not allow ye States to be independent, will be without Hesitation rejected." Etc.

199 Gerry, Elbridge. A. L. S. 4to. 4 pp. Philadelphia, June 27, 1777. To John Wendell.

"The spirit shewn by ye Jersey Militia upon ye Movement of General Howe, is a favourable Circumstance to our affairs, & greatly tends to intimidate our Enemies, he marched with but part of his Army to Somerset Court House, about ten Miles from Brunswick in Hopes of tempting our General to immediate Action, but this being avoided, untill a Body of Troops that were posted at peeks Kill could reinforce our Army & ye Militia be Collected, Mr. Howe then tho't it not for his Interest to risque a Battle, and retired to Amboy, had General Washington left his post, to have attacked General Howe, ye latter might have slowly retreated towards Brunswick, untill joined by ye residue of his Troops, & then ye Combat. would have been nearly with equal Numbers on each side, and might have been hazardous; but when reinforced as before mentioned, I think G— Was— had a promising prospect of defeating ye Enemy.

"An attack may be expected on Tyconderoga; I hope ye New Hampshire Battalions have their Complement of Men, or that their Deficiency is supplyed with Militia, as ye carrying that post may give spirit to ye Enemy & bring ye War neare to our Door; altho I really think it would not be much injurious to our cause." Etc.

200 Gerry, Elbridge. A. L. S. 4to. 3 pp. Philadelphia, Jan. 10, 1780.

201 Gerry, Elbridge. A. L. S. Folio. 3 pp. Philadelphia, May 16, 1780. To John Wendell.

"The Marquis de Lafayette arrived in this City ye last Evening & I had ye Pleasure of a visit from him with letters from our friends Mr. Adams and Mr. Dana. They are agreably situated in Paris, waiting ye events of War to produce an Alteration in ye mad Disposition of ye Ministry of G. Britain which nothing but misfortune can alter." * * * "Charleston was safe on ye 20th of April, but General Lincoln informed ye Governor of Virginia, that Troops were wanted." Etc.

202 Gerry, Elbridge. A. L. S. 4to. Cambridge, November 16, 1787. To John Wendell.

"If the new Constitution should be adopted I shall think it my duty to support it, but as it now stands I think it neither consistent with the principles of the Revolution, or of the Constitutions of the several States, & it is condemned by the best Writers on free Governments, indeed the eastern States will soon rebel against it, for it is not a Government adapted to their Genius, Habits, or aversion to arbitrary power, but if they are of a different opinion, I have no objection to their trying on the fœderal chains, for such I am persuaded they will find the bonds of this constitution eventually to be. This *entre nous*." Etc.

203 Gerry, Elbridge. A. L. S. Folio. 3 pp. New York, July 4, 1790. To John Wendell. With address.

"The uneasiness of the people arises more from a disappointment of the immediate benefits they were promised from the operation of the new Constitution, than from other causes, I always predicted discontent from this cause, for when the proper line of policy was to prepare the people at the time they were ratifying the Constitution, for a patient submission to the Administration thereof until the good effects could be attained, they were elated with promises that as soon as the government could be put in motion commerce, manufactures & agriculture would flourish, the value of lands would be enhanced, the public debts would be funded, money would be plenty, &c &c &c & their inevitable disappointment produces uneasiness." Etc.

204 Gerry, Elbridge. A. L. S. 4to. 3 pp. Cambridge, Jan.
12, 1799. To John Wendell. With address.

"I will give Boston the credit, of being a place the most inimical to
me of any on the globe, the office which I lately filled, contrary to my
wishes, was probably sought for by one of a party in that & a neigh-
bouring town, who have been always my antipodes; and for what
reasons, I know not, unless for my original sins of Independence." Etc.

205 H EYWARD, THOS. D. S. Folio. Charleston, Sep.
11, 1787.

The document written and signed by Jacob Reed, member of the
Continental Congress.

206 Hopkins, Stephen. D. S. 4to. Oct., 1771

207 Huntington, Sam'l. President of the Continental Congress;
Governor of Connecticut. L. S. Folio. 2 pp. Philada.,
Oct. 9, 1779. To the Governor of Georgia.

Signed as President of the Continental Congress.

208 Huntington, Sam'l. D. S. Folio. 2 pp. Philada., March
11, 1780. Attested by Chas. Thomson, Sec'y of Congress.

Proclamation appointing April 26, 1780, as a day of fasting, humili-
ation and prayer.

209 J EFFERSON, THOMAS. Third President of the United
States. Author of the Declaration of Independence.
A. L. S. 4to. Philada., July 1, 1792. To James
Brown. With franked address.

210 Jefferson, Thos. A. D. S. (bank check). April 5, 1793.

211 L IVINGSTON, PHILIP. D. S. Folio. New York,
June 3, 1790.

Attesting, as one of the committee appointed to decide the election of
State Senators, to the election of Peter Lefferts and others. Signed
also by Sam'l Jones, James Gordon, Peter Vanderwoort, Isaac Roosevelt,
Matthew Clarkson, Abraham Bancker, Paul Micheau and others.

212 M ORRIS, ROBERT. Financier during the Revolution. A. L. S. 4to. July 14, 1795.

213 Morris, Robert. A. D. 2 pp. 4to. N. P., N. D.

214 Morris, Robert. D. S. Small 4to. Philadelphia, Aug. 14,
1779.

"I do hereby engage to be answerable to the Library Company of
Philadelphia, for the time of one year, for any Books which may be
lent to John Swanwick."

215 Morris, Robert. A. N. S. With initials, 4to, and D. S.,
4to. V. D.   2 pieces.

216 Morton, John. Signature on a piece of Pennsylvania Colonial Paper Money. 1772

217 PACA, WILLIAM. A. D. S. (twice). Large folio. 2 pp.
Dec. 14, 1771.

218 Paca, William. Parchment D. S. Folio. March 12, 1785.
Signed also by John Rogers, Chancellor of Maryland.

219 Paine, Robert Treat. Autograph Inscription. Small 4to.
"Rob.-Treat Paine's Singing Book; began February 7,
1748. E. M., Tutor."

The inscription on the leaf "from Robert Treat Paine's Singing Book,"
is in Old English capital letters, surrounded with many fancy flourishes
of the pen, forming a very interesting memento of his schoolboy days.

220 Paine, Robert Treat. A. D. S. Folio. 2 pp. Feb. 5, 1780.
Legal document, signed as Attorney-General of Massachusetts.

221 Paine, Robert Treat. A. D. S. Folio. 2 pp. Feb. 5, 1780.
Legal document, signed as Attorney-General of Massachusetts.

222 READ, GEORGE. A. D. S. 2 pp. Feb., 1771.

223 Read, George. D. S. Folio. Dec. 20, 1777.
Resolution of the House of Assembly of the State of Delaware.

224 Rodney, Cæsar. D. S. 4to. New Castle, Oct. 25, 1772.
To Richard Penn. With address.

A petition to Richard Penn, Lieutenant-Governor of Delaware and
Pennsylvania, for the life of a criminal, sentenced to death for burg-
lary. Signed also by Richard W. William and David Hall.

225 Ross, George. Autograph Extract. Signed. From the
diary of Conrad Weiser. Folio. 1760.

Fine specimen.

"The following anecdote I extracted from the diary of Conrad Weiser,
Esq., wrote in his own hand, July 3d:—

'The two Indians told me that the French Indian (so they called
him) that was last Winter in Philad. pretending to be a Messenger
from the Ohio Indians, reported on his return, that the Quakers in
Philad'a. gave him a rod for the Indians in Ohio to chastise the people
Setling on the Indians' Lands on the other side the Apalatein Mountains and to take Courage. The Majority of the People of Pensil'va was
on the Indian side of the Question and do disapprooff (sic) of the Proceedings of Onas in Selling the Indian County.'   G. Ross."

226 Rutledge, Edward. Governor of South Carolina. A. L. S.
4to. 2 pp. N. P., N. D. To William H. Gibbs. With
address.

Fine specimen. Containing also an A. L. S., with (initials) of Chancellor H. W. Desaussure, dated Jan. 24, 1800, conveying the intelligence of the death of Edward Rutledge. "He had a presentment of
his death, immediately after the arrival of the intelligence of the death
of our great Washington, for whom he deeply mourned." Etc.

227 Rutledge, Edward. D. S. Folio. Charleston, June 13,
1788. Signed also by John f. Grimke, Colonel in the
Revolutionary War, and by Jacob Read, Member of the
Old Congress.

1761. The following Anecdote I extracted from the
diary of Conrad Weiser Esq: written in his
own hand —

July
3:

"The two Indians told me that the French had
"Indian (so they called him) that was but a
"Winter in Phila: pretending to be a
"Winter from the Ohio Indians - Phila:
"Messenger from the Ohio Indians ... Phila
"on his return that the Indians on Ohio
"gave him a ... for the people settling on the
"to chastise the people on the other sides the Appalachin
"Indians Lands on the other side the Appalachin
"Mountains and to take Congress the Majority
"of the people of Provil ... do disapprove
"of the People of Provil and to disapprove of
"... of the Question and to disapprove
"... of the proceedings of ... in selling
"of the Indian Country —

G. Nolk

228 Rush, Benjamin. A. L. S. 4to. Sept. 22, 1780; and
A. N. S., small 4to. March 12, 1779. 2 pieces.
Both orders on the Philadelphia Library for books.

229 SHERMAN, ROGER. A. D. S. 4to. Jan., 1757.
Fine specimen. Signed as Justice of the Peace of New Milford.

230 THORNTON, MATTHEW. A. D. S. Folio. April
11, 1762.

231 WALTON, GEORGE. D. S. Folio. N. P., N. D.

232 Whipple, William. D. S. 4to. March 26, 1782.
Signed as Speaker of the House of Representatives of New Hampshire.

233 Williams, William. D. S., (and partly written). Folio.
Nov. 13, 1795.

234 Wilson, James. D. S. Folio. Jan. 14, 1795.

235 Walcott, Oliver. A. L. S. 4to. Litchfield, May 24, 1755.
To Jared Ingersoll, of New Haven.
Fine specimen.

236 Wythe, George. A. L. S., in the third person. 4to.
Oct. 31, 1801. To E. Robinson. With address.
" G. Wythe to E. Robinson.
" I thank thee, good sir, for thy kind letter received yesterday, and
shall be obliged to thee for endeavouring to preserve my land and
house from devastation until i can sell or lease them, i beg thee to present my good wishes to my friend and old acquaintance thy father,
adieu, 31 Octob, 1801."

237 Wythe, Geo. D. S. Folio. N. P., N. D.
Legal document. Signed also by Governor Botetourt, of Virginia.

MEMBERS OF THE CONSTITUTIONAL CONVENTION.

238 BASSETT, RICHARD. A. D. S. Folio. N. P., N. D.

239 Bedford, Gunning. A. D. S. Small 4to. April 9, 1804.

240 Brearley, David. A. L. S. 4to. Jan. 12, 1784. To Gov. Livingston.

241 DICKINSON, JOHN. Author of the "Farmer's Letters." A. L. S. 4to. 2 pp. Fairhill, Aug. 23, 1774. To Jas. Wilson. With address.

242 Dickinson, John. A. L. S. 4to. 2 pp. To Rev. Sam'l Miller. With address.

243 ELLSWORTH, OLIVER. Chief Justice of the U. S. A. D. With signature in the body. Small 4to. Hartford, Dec. 2, 1783.

244 Ellsworth, Oliver. A. L. S. (Signature attached). Paris, Aug. 15, 1800.

245 GERRY, ELBRIDGE. Signer of the Declaration of Independence. A. L. S. 4to. 3 pp. Cambridge, Sep. 28, 1799. To Jno. Wendell.

> "That we had cause of war & a right to declare it, before I went to France as well as at the present time cannot be denied; but if it was good policy then, it is equally so now, to establish peace if possible, on just & honorable terms if these cannot be obtained, on a fair tryal, my individual voice is for War."

246 Gerry, Elbridge. A. L. S. 4to. 8 pp. Cambridge, Jan. 12, 1801. To John Wendell.

> Very interesting letter on the political condition of the country at the time.

247 Gilman, Nicholas. A. L. S. 4to. Exeter, Feb. 2, 1781.

248 JENIFER, DAN'L, OF ST. THOMAS. A. L. S. 4to. Annapolis, Dec. 2, 1766. To Rob't Christie. With address.

249 LANSING, JOHN. A. L. S. Folio. Aug. 19, 1785.

250 Lansing, John. A. L. S. Folio. 2 pp. June 26, 1786. To Jeremiah Van Rensselaer. With address.

251 Lansing, John. A. D. S. Folio. July 12, 1781.

252 Livingston, Wm. Brig.-Gen. in the Revolutionary War and Governor of New Jersey. A. D. S. Folio. N. P., N. D.

253 Livingston, Wm. D. S. Folio. Burlington, Oct. 13, 1779.

254 MARTIN, LUTHER. A. L. S. Folio. N. P., N. D.

255 Martin, Luther. A. D. S. Folio. March 5, 1795.

256 PENDLETON, NATHANIEL. A. L. S. 4to. 2 pp.
Catskill, Nov. 8, 1811. With address.
General Hamilton's second in the duel with Colonel Burr.

257 Pickering, John. A. L. S. 4to. Portsmouth, Jan. 2, 1788.

258 Pinckney, Charles. A. L. S. 4to. Oct. 6, 1802.

259 Pinckney, Charles Cotesworth, A. D. S. Folio. Jan. 4.
1774. Signed also by Thos. Bee, Member of the Old
Congress, and Henry Pendleton, Judge of the Supreme
Court.

260 Pinckney, Charles Cotesworth. A. D. S. Small 4to. Aug.
2, 1802. Inlaid.

261 YATES, ROBERT. A. D. S. 4to. Albany, Nov. 5,
1773.

262 Yates, Robert. A. L. S. Folio. Albany, April 9, 1773.
To John T. Kemp. With address.

263 Yates, Robert. A. D., folio, and D. S., 4to. 1772. 2 pieces.

OFFICERS IN THE REVOLUTIONARY WAR.

264 ABORN, SAMUEL. Colonel in the Revolution. A. L. S.
Small 4to. To Sam'l Aborn, Jr.
" Let the bearer, Levi Aldrich, have a quarter of a yard of broad
cloath & 14 Buttons."

265 Angell, Israel. Colonel in the Revolution. A. L. S. 4to.
Johnston, May 29, 1793. To Welcom Arnold. With
address.

266 Armstrong, John. Served in the Revolution under Mercer
and Gates. Brigadier-General in the War of 1812.
A. L. S. 4to. War Dept., July 19, 1814.

267 Arnold, John. Colonel in the Revolution. D. S. Folio.
1807.

268 Arnold, John. D. S., and two lines autograph. Small
4to. Warwich, Oct. 5, 1808.

269 BALL, JOSEPH. Prisoner on board the prison-ship "Torbay." Small 4to. March 14, 1767.

270 Barry, John. Distinguished Captain in the Continental Navy. First Commodore of the United States. D. S. 4to. N. P., N. D.

271 Beard, Jonas. Distinguished Colonel in the Revolutionary War. A. L. S. 4to. Feb. 20, 1788. To Col. Rich'd Hamton. With address.

272 Beekman, B. Colonel in the Revolution. A. L. S. 4to. Camp at Sheldon, Aug. 23, 1779. To Lieut.-Colonel Grimke. With address.

273 Berrien, John. Major in the Revolution. A. L. S. 4to. 3 pp. Savannah, Dec. 1, 1786.

274 Berrien, John. A. L. S. Folio. 2 pp. Louisville, Jan. 13, 1797.

275 Biddle, Clement. Col. in the Revolution. A. L. S. 4to. Phila., Aug. 21, 1783. To Gen. Mifflin. With address. Refers to the services of Colonel Henry Hollingsworth.

276 Blundell, Nathaniel. Prisoner on board the prison-ship "Torbay." A. D. S. Small 4to. Aug. 14, 1761.

277 Braham, Ferdinand de. Major in the Revolution. A. D. S. 4to., and D. S., small 4to. Feb. 11, 1782. 2 pieces

278 Breckinridge, Alex. Captain in the Revolution and early Kentucky pioneer. A. D. S. 4to. 1797.

279 Bullitt, Alex. S. Colonel in the Revolution and Kentucky pioneer. A. L. S. 4to. June 23, 1788.

280 Burke, Ædanus. Soldier of the Revolution. Justice of the Supreme Court of South Carolina. Published a pamphlet on the Society of the Cincinnati. A. L. S. 4to. 2 pp. Charlestown, June 28, 1783. To Gen. McIntosh. With address.

281 Burr, Aaron. Colonel in the Revolution, Vice-President of the U. S., and killed Alex. Hamilton in a duel. A. L. S. 4to. With address.

282 Burrows, W. W. Major in the Revolution. A. L. S. 4to. July 5, 1784, and A. D. S., small 4to. 2 pieces

283 CADWALADER, JOHN. Brigadier-General in the Revolution. A. L. S. 4to. Jan. 8, 1786. Fine specimen. Rare.

284 Cadwalader, Lambert. Officer in the Revolution. Member of the Old Congress from New Jersey. D. S. 4to. Jan. 29, 1817.

285 Call, Richard. Colonel in the Revolution. A. L. S. Folio. Camp Shoulderbone, October 29, 1786.

286 Call, Richard. Part of A. L. S. 4to.

287 Campbell, John. Officer in the Revolution. A. L. S. 4to. July 11, 1776.

288 Claiborne, Richard. Major in the Revolution. A. L. S. Folio. Philadelphia, October 23, 1780. With address.

289 Claiborne, Richard. A. L. S. 4to. N. P., N. D.

290 Claus, Daniel. Colonel in the Revolution. A. L. S. 4to. Williamsburg, Nov. 7, 1770. To Sir Wm. Johnson, Bart.

291 Claus, Daniel. A. L. S. 4to. Williamsburg, Nov. 13, 1768. To Sir Wm. Johnson, Bart.

292 Cole, Edward. Colonel in the French and Indian War. A. L. S. 4to. Newport, Aug. 25, 1770.

293 DÉLLIENT, A. Celebrated Officer in the Revolutionary War. A. L. S. 4to. Charlestown, Feb. 28, 1783; and A. D. S., small 4to., May 6, 1782.

294 Dickinson, Philemon. Commanded the New Jersey Militia at Monmouth. Member of the Old Congress. A. L. S. 4to. 3 pp. Trenton, Aug. 5, 1782.

295 Dougherty, H. Captain in the Revolution. L. S. Folio. Liberty Island, Nov. 16, 1775. To the Committee of Safety for the City and Liberties of Philadelphia.

296 EUSTAU, J. S. Brave Officer in the Revolution. Aide to Generals Lee and Green. Brig.-Gen. in the French Army. A. N. S. Small 4to. No date.

297 FANNING, EDWARD. Tory Colonel in the Revolution. D. S. 4to. July 30, 1772.

298 Fish, Nicholas. Distinguished Colonel in the Revolution. A. D. S. 4to. New York, May 15, 1787.
General orders for General Fisher's brigade.

299 GARDNER, LEWIS. Colonel in the Revolution. A. L. S. 4to. Georgia, Columbia Co., Oct. 16, 1791.

300 Gage, Thomas. British General. Sent the expedition to Concord, in 1775, which caused the Battle of Lexington. Governor of Massachusetts Colony. L. S. Folio. New York, July 2, 1766. To Governor Penn, of Pennsylvania.
Interesting letter in reference to the punishment of settlers for killing Indians and encroaching on their lands.

301 Gibbes, W. Hasell. Capt. in the Revolution; was at the Siege of Savannah; exiled to St. Augustine. A. D. S. 4to. Jan. 28, 1804.

302 Gillon, A. Commodore in the Navy of the Revolution. A. L. S. Folio. 3 pp. Charleston, Oct. 8, 1783.

303 Gillon, A. A. L. S. 4to. No date.

304 Grimke, J. f. Distinguished Colonel in the Revolution and Judge. A. L. S. 4to. Charleston, May 30, 1800.

305 HALL, D. Colonel in the Revolution. Governor of Delaware. A. L. S. 4to. 3 pp. Lewes, Nov. 28, 1804.

306 Hall, D. A. D. S. 4to, Dec. 28, 1804.

307 Harrison, Robert H. Distinguished Officer in the Revolution, Aide and Military Secretary to General Washington. A. L. S. Folio. Head Quarters, May 20, 1780. To Brig.-Gen. Maxwell, at Elizabethtown. With address.

308 Hart, Wm. General in the Revolution. L. S. 4to. Say Brooke, Sept. 10, 1802,

309 Haskell, E. Officer in the Revolution. A. L. S. (twice). 4to. Jan, 12, 1782.

310 Henry, John. Captain in the Revolution. " The Spy." A. L. S. 4to. Boston, Dec, 18, 1806. With address.

311 Houstoun, James. Surgeon in the Continental Army. A. L. S. Folio. 2 pp. Philadelphia, June, 2, 1777. To Gen. McIntosh.

> " General Washington by the best accounts I can obtain has about 12,000 men, and more arriving daily from Southard, he has moved his headquarters on Monday last to a place called Bound broke which is not many miles from Brunswick, our troops are in high spirits, and have little skimishes with the Enemy almost every day.
> " Governor Tryon and Col. Walcot, with about 500 men lost their lives in that excursion they made into England." Etc., etc.

312 Houstoun, James. A. L. S. 4to. 2 pp. Savannah, Jan. 25, 1783. To Jacob Read. With address.

313 Howell, John. Officer in the Revolution. A. L. S. 4to. Augusta, Sep. 25, 1790. To Gen. Lachlan McIntosh. With address.

314 Huntington, Jedediah. Brig.-Gen. in the Revolution. A. L. S. (with initials). 4to. Dec. 13, 1793.

315 IRVINE, WM. Brig.-Gen. in the Revolution. Member of the Old Congress. D. S. 4to. Phila., May, 30, 1804.

316 Irwin, John. Colonel in the Revolution. A. L. S. Folio. Pittsburg, July 10, 1783. With address.

317 JONES, JOHN. Officer in the Revolution. A. L. S. 4to. 2 pp. Spent Creek, May 21, 1780. To Gov. Richard Howley. With address.

> " Tis whispered about this quarter as a Secret that Charlestown is taken by the British troops and that a large party of 'em is dayly expected to Augusta, this Sir gives me fresh Occation to press you for Amunition of which I trust you will send as much you shall think sufficient for 45 and the most of them fighting men." Etc.

318 KNOX, HENRY. Major-Gen. in the Revolution, and first Secretary of the Society of the Cincinnati. L. S. Folio. War Department, March 9, 1791.

319 LOWNDES, RAWLINS. Noted patriot during the Revolution and President of South Carolina. A. L. S. Folio. Charles Town, Jan. 21, 1779. To Governor Houston. With address.

Very interesting letter in reference to the critical condition of the county (Georgia), and recommending means to overcome the enemy.

320 Lowndes, Rawlins. A. L. S. Folio. 2 pp. Charleston, Aug. 22, 1792. To Ralph Izard. With address.

321 Lushington, R. Colonel in the Revolution. A. L. S. 4to. Charleston, June 19, 1788.

322 MARBURY, LEONARD. Colonel in the Revolution. A. L. S. 4to. St. Mary's, Nov. 29, 1790. With address.

323 Mathews, Geo. Col. in the Revolution. Wounded at Brandywine. Governor of Georgia. D. S. Folio. Sep. 16, 1795.

324 Mayson, James. Colonel in the Revolution. A. L. S. Folio. Aug. 10, 1789. To Peter Freneau. With address.

325 Mifflin, Thos. Maj.-Gen. in the Revolutionary War, Signer of the Constitution and Gov. of Pennsylvania. D. S. 4to. Philada., Dec. 30, 1786, and A. D. S., small 4to. 2 pieces

326 Miles, Saml. Col. in the Revolution. A. L. S. Folio. 2 pp. Philada., Nov. 25, 1780. To Joseph Reed. With address.

327 Milledge, John. Officer in the Revolution, Gov. of Georgia and President *pro tem.* of the Senate. A. L. S., folio, Washington, April 30, 1802, and A. D. S., 4to., Jan. 12, 1778. 2 pieces

328 Morris, Jacob. Distinguished officer in the Revolution and aide to Gen. Chas. Lee. A. L. S., 4to., 2 pp., Butternuts, May 21, 1806, with address; and A. L. S., 4to, April 7, 1805, with address. 2 pieces

329 O'FALLON, JAMES. Surgeon in the Revolution. A. L. S. 4to. Louisville, Feb. 14, 1792. With address.

330 PARKER, RICHARD. Colonel in the Revolution. A. L. S. Folio. 2 pp. N. P., N. D.

331 Palmer, J. Officer in the Revolution. A. L. S. Folio. Braintree, Dec. 5, 1777.

"The General (Spencer) has also charged me with occasioning the failure of the R'd Island Expedition. This will occasion my being tried by a Court Martial."

332 Pannill, Jospeh. Lieut.-Col. of the Georgia Line in the Revolution. A. L. S., 4to., 2 pp., Wilkes, May 17, 1785; A. L. S., 4to, Wilkes, July 12, 1784.   2 pieces

333 Parsons, Sam'l H. Major-Gen. in the Revolution. Justice Northwestern Territory. A. L. S. Folio. Falls of Ohio, Dec. 8, 1785.

334 Parsons, Sam'l H. A. L. S. · 4to. Hartford, June, 1780.
Interesting military letter.

335 Patton, John. Colonel in the Revolution. Radnor Meeting House, March 18, 1778.
Interesting letter, narrating a skirmish with the enemy at the Fox Chase.

336 Pawling, Albert. Colonel· in the Revolution. A. L. S., 4to., Jan. 30, 1806; and A. L. S., New York, Jan. 14, 1806.   2 pieces

337 Pinckney, Chas. Cotesworth. Brevet Brig.-Gen. in the Revolution, Aide to Gen. Washington, Signer of the Constitution. A. L. S. 4to. 4 pp. Charleston, March 10, 1793.

338 Pinckney, Chas. Cotesworth. Two A. D's. S. 4tos. 2 pieces.

339 Pinckney, Thos. Major-General U. S. Army, Aide to Gen. Lincoln in the Revolution, Governor of S. C. A. L. S. 4to. Charleston, Nov. 6, 1776. With address.

340 Pinckney, Thos. A. L. S. 4to. Nov. 29, 1815; two A. L. S., in the third person, 4tos, Oct. 20, 1787, and no date; L. S., 4to, Jan. 28, 1815, and D. S., folio, Jan. 1, 1784.   5 pieces

341 Platt, Richard. Colonel in the Revolution. A. L. S. 4to. 2 pp. April 14, 1807. With address.

342 Pomeroy, Ralph. Commissioner of clothing in the Revolution. A. L. S. Folio. Phila., April, 13, 1779.

343 Putnam, Rufus. General in the Revolution and Judge of the Northwest Territory. A. L. S. 4to. Rutland, Oct. 10, 1786. With address.
Rare.

344 REED, JOSEPH. Brig.-Gen. in the Revolution and President of Penna. L. S. 4to. Phila., May 27, 1780.

345 Reed, Jos. A. L. S. Folio. 3 pp. July 23, 1781. To David Duncan, Fort Pitt.
Interesting letter in reference to Fort Pitt and Gen. Clark's Expedition.

346 Roberdeau, Daniel. Distinguished Officer in the Revolution, Member of the Old Congress. A. L. S. 4to. 4 pp. Phila., Sept. 27, 1784. (Damaged).

347 Rogers, Hezekiah. Officer in the Revolution. A. L. S. 4to. War Dept., Sept. 4, 1804.

348 Rogers, Wm. Chaplain in the Revolutionary Army. Professor in the University of Penna. A. L. S. 4to. 2 pp. Phila., April 5, 1818.

349 Root, Jesse. Col. in the Revolution, Member of the Old Congress. A. L. S. 4to. Hartford, Jan. 27, 1804. With address.

350 SAVAGE, THOMAS. Member of the Council of Safety of Savannah; exiled to St. Augustine in 1780. A. L. S. Folio. 2 pp. Dec. 14, 1775.

> "The late Congress contrary to my Inclination (knowing my Inability) has made me the 13th part of a General by appointing me One of the Council of Safety, at which Board I am constantly from 9 in the morning till 4 or 5 in the afternoon. * * * * As to my own part I am Determined to Defend as far in my Power Lies the Liberties of America." Etc., etc.

351 Savage, Thomas. A. L's. S., 4tos, April 26, 1784, and March 11, 1775; folio, March 10, 1775, and D. S., small 4to. 4 pieces.

352 Sherburne, John. Major in the Revolution, U. S. District Judge. A. L. S. 4to. Aug. 13, 1792.

353 Skinner, Cortland. Tory Brig.-Gen. in the Revolution. D. S. 4to. Oct. 12, 1767. Signed also by Frederick Smyth, Chief Justice of the Province of New Jersey.

354 Smallman, Thomas. Major in the Revolution. A. L. S. Folio. Pittsburg, June 16, 1773. With address.

> Relating to goods delivered to Capt. "White Eyes."

355 Smith, Wm. S. Aide to Gen. Washington. A. L. S. Small 4to. March 7, 1800.

356 Spencer, Joseph. Maj.-Gen. in the Revolution. Served in the War of 1756. Member of the Old Congress and Judge of the S. C. of Conn. D. S. Folio. Providence, Dec. 31, 1777.

357 Spencer, Oliver. Col. in the Revolution, Judge in the Northwest Territory. Folio. Columbia, Sept. 24, 1791.

358 Stevenson, James. Officer in the Revolution. A. L. S. 4to, 2 pp., Niagara, Oct. 19, 1769, and A. D. S., 4to, Albany, Feb. 21, 1765. 2 pieces.

359 Sullivan, John. Major-General in the Revolutionary War. Attorney-General of New Hampshire. A. D. S. Folio. Feb. 19, 1773.

360 TEMPLE, BENJ. Colonel in the Revolution. A. L. S. Folio. 2 pp. King William, April 21, 1779. To Col. Theodorick Bland. With address.

361 Templeton, Andrew. Captain in the Revolution. A. D. S. 4to. April 25, 1780.

362 Thomson, Wm. Commanded at Sullivan's Island. A. L. S.
4to. N. P., N. P.

In reference to the distribution of the medals of the Society of the Cincinnati.

363 Thomson, Wm. Three A. D's. S. Small 8vos. 1777,
1778 and 1786. 3 pieces

364 Thomson, W. R. Officer in the Revolution. A. D. S.
Folio. Oct. 1, 1795.

365 Trumbull, Jonathan. Officer in the Revolution. Senior
aide to Genl. Washington. Governor of Connecticut.
A. D. S. 4to. 2 pp. Sep. 18, 1788. Signed also by
Eliphalet Dyer, member of the Old Congress.

366 Tryon, Moses. Captain in the Navy of the Revolution.
A. L. S., folio, New London, Sep. 1, 1799 ; and A. L. S.,
4to, Jan. 7, 1802. 2 pieces

367 Twiggs John. Brig.-Gen. in the Revolution. A. L. S., 4to,
N. P., N. D. ; and A. L. S., 4to (damaged). 2 pieces

368 VARICK, RICHARD. Distinguished Colonel in the
Revolution. Military Secretary and Aide to Gen.
Washington. A. L. S. 4to. Jersey, May 1. 1825.
With address.

369 Varick, Richard. A. L. S., folio, New York, Dec. 18, 1821,
and A. D. S., 4to, March 30, 1822. 2 pieces

370 WADELL, HENRY. Tory in the Revolution. A.
L. S. 4to. Freehold, April 11, 1777.

In answer to a summons to appear before the Council of Safety of New Jersey, he being suspected of being dangerous to the Government.

371 Wickly, John. Officer in the Revolution. A. L. S. 4to.
Aug. 7, 1790.

372 Williams, Jonathan. Brig.-Gen. in the Revolution. A. L. S.
4to. 4 pp. Nantes, July 11, 1777.

373 Whistler, Major John. Officer in the Revolution, under
Burgoyne. Built Fort Dearborn, Chicago. A. L. S.
Folio. Fort Dearborn, Sep. 13, 1808. (Stained).

374 YATES, CHAS. P. Colonel in the Revolution. A. L. S.
4to. Jan. 18, 1790.

COLONIAL GOVERNORS.

375 ANDROS, SIR EDMUND, of New York.   D. S.   Folio. New York, April 9, 1680.   Laid down.

Commission of Tunnis de Kay, appointing him Ensign of Militia.

376 BEEKMAN, GERARDUS, of New York.   1710.   Part of L. S.   4to.

Signed also by Rip Van Dam, Colonial Governor of New York, in 1731.

377 Belcher, Jonathan, of Massachusetts, 1730, and of New Jersey.   A. L. S.   4to.   Boston, Oct. 5, 1741.

Letter of condolence to Secretary Waldron.

378 Belcher, Jonathan.   D. S.   4to.   Burlington, Feb. 12, 1752.

379 Belcher, Jonathan.   D. S.   4to.   Aug. 10, 1752.

380 Bellingham, Richard, of Massachusetts.   1641, 1654 and 1655.   A. L. S.   4to.   Boston, June 17, no year.   With address.

381 Bradstreet, Simon, of Massachusetts.   1679-1686.   A. D. S. (twice).   April 9, 1676.

382 DANFORTH, THOS.   Deputy Governor of Massachu-setts.   A. D. S.   4to.   May 14, 1672.

383 Dudley, Joseph, of Massachusetts.   1714, 1715.   D. S. (twice).   Folio.   2 pp.   Portsmouth, Oct. 8, 1708.

The accounts of Samuel Penhallow (and signed by him), Treasurer and Receiver General of Her Majesty's Revenues within the Province of New Hampshire, for the years 1707 and 1708.   Samuel Penhallow was the author of the " History of the Indian Wars."

384 Dudley, Joseph.   A. L. S.   4to.   Boston, June 11, 1711. To Secretary Story.   With franked address.

385 EDEN, SIR ROBERT, of Maryland.   1769–1774.   D. S.   4to.   Folio.   April 26, 1775.

386 Ellis, Henry, of Georgia.   1757–1760.   D. S.   4to.   Savan-nah, July 7, 1760.

387 FITCH, THOS., of Connecticut.   1754–1766.   A. L. S. Folio.   2pp.   Norwalk, Sept. 28, 1767.

Fine specimen.

388 Fletcher, Benj., of New York, 1692.   D. S.   Folio.   New York, February 9, 1692-3.   Broken in the folds.

Captain's commission.

389 GREENE, WM., of Rhode Island. 1743-1758. D. S.
Folio. Aug. 29, 1748.
Commission of Samuel Aborn, as lieutenant.

390 Greene, Wm., of Rhode Island. 1778 to 1786. A. L. S.
4to. Nov. 10, 1783.

391 Greene, Wm. A. L. S. 4to. Feb. 8, 1799. With address.

392 Greene, Wm. D. S. Folio. June 17, 1774. Signed also
by Josiah Lyndon, Colonial Governor; Henry Ward,
Colonial Governor; Metcalf Bowler, Member of the
Stamp Act Congress, and Nathan Miller, Member of
the Old Congress.

393 MORRIS, ROBT. H., of Pennsylvania. A. L. S. 4to.
Philada., Dec. 17, 1754. To Gov. Sharpe, of Maryland.

394 NANFAN, JOHN, of New York. 1699-1701. A.D.S.
4to. July 27, 1700. Signed also by Abraham De
Peyster, Chief Justice.

395 PEPPERRELL, SIR WM. Acting Governor of Massa-
chusetts. Portion of D. S. Folio. June 3, 1757.
Signed also by all the members of the Massachusetts
Council.

396 SALTONSTALL, GURDON, of Connecticut. 1708-1725.
A. D. S. 4to. May 17, 1708.

397 Sharpe, Horatio, of Maryland. Bill of Exchange, endorsed.
Nov. 14, 1763.

398 Shirley, Wm., of Massachusetts. 1741-1753. A. L. S.
4to. Dec., 1755. To Hon. Robt. Hunter.
In reference to the settlement of Indian affairs.

399 Shirley, Wm. A. L. S. 4to. Nov. 18, 1748. With address to Sir Wm. Pepperrell.

400 Shirley, Wm. D. S. Commission. Folio. June 10, 1755.
With seal.

401 TALCOTT, JOSEPH, of Connecticut. 1725-1742. D. S.
Folio. Sept. 14, 1725.

402 Trumbull, Jonathan, of Connecticut. 1769-1784. A. D. S.
Folio. July 8, 1778.

403 USHER, JOHN. Lieut.-Gov. of New Hampshire. A.
D. S. Small 4to. Newcastle, Sept. 5, 1705.

404 Usher, John. D. S. 4to. Portsmouth, Nov. 23, 1703.

Gurdon Saltonstall Esqr Govr of her
Majtys Colony of Connecticut.

To Capt Mathew Allin of Windsor

Thefe are to Signifie, that upon Application to me
made, by Capt Benjamin Now beny's Safign in Mr
Company to be difcharged from that Post
I found granted him liberty to lay down his Commiffion
for yt Post, in Confideration of his having been known
Since with a Captain Commiffion, & servd his Commiffion
faithfully in yt Station. You are therfore to purfue

389 GREENE, WM., of Rhode Island. 1743–1758. D. S. Folio. Aug. 29, 1748.

Commission of Samuel Aborn, as lieutenant.

390 Greene, Wm., of Rhode Island. 1778 to 1786. A. L. S. 4to. Nov. 10, 1783.

391 Greene, Wm. A. L. S. 4to. Feb. 8, 1799. With address.

392 Greene, Wm. D. S. Folio. June 17, 1774. Signed also by Josiah Lyndon, Colonial Governor; Henry Ward, Colonial Governor; Metcalf Bowler, Member of the Stamp Act Congress, and Nathan Miller, Member of the Old Congress.

393 MORRIS, ROBT. H., of Pennsylvania. A. L. S. 4to. Philada., Dec. 17, 1754. To Gov. Sharpe, of Maryland.

394 NANFAN, JOHN, of New York. 1699–1701. A. D. S. 4to. July 27, 1700. Signed also by Abraham De Peyster, Chief Justice.

395 PEPPERRELL, SIR WM. Acting Governor of Massachusetts. Portion of D. S. Folio. June 3, 1757. Signed also by all the members of the Massachusetts Council.

396 SALTONSTALL, GURDON, of Connecticut. 1708–1725. A. D. S. 4to. May 17, 1708.

397 Sharpe, Horatio, of Maryland. Bill of Exchange, endorsed. Nov. 14, 1763.

398 Shirley, Wm., of Massachusetts. 1741–1753. A. L. S. 4to. Dec., 1755. To Hon. Robt. Hunter.

In reference to the settlement of Indian affairs.

399 Shirley, Wm. A. L. S. 4to. Nov. 18, 1748. With address to Sir Wm. Pepperrell.

400 Shirley, Wm. D. S. Commission. Folio. June 10, 1755. With seal.

401 TALCOTT, JOSEPH, of Connecticut. 1725–1742. D. S. Folio. Sept. 14, 1725.

402 Trumbull, Jonathan, of Connecticut. 1769–1784. A. D. S. Folio. July 8, 1778.

403 USHER, JOHN. Lieut.-Gov. of New Hampshire. A. D. S. Small 4to. Newcastle, Sept. 5, 1705.

404 Usher, John. D. S. 4to. Portsmouth, Nov. 23, 1703.

Gurdon Saltonstall Esqr Govr of her
Majties Colony of Connecticot.

To Capt Mathew Allin of Windsor

Wheras are to signifie, that upon Application to me
made, by Capt Benjamin Newbery Esqr of Wth
Company to be discharged from that Post he is
I have granted him liberty to lay down his Commission
for ye Post, in Consideraon of his having been known
Since with a Captain Commissn, & so end his Commissn
faithfully in ye Station. You are therfore to proceed
to supply ye Vacancy so made, by Vertue on Instign,
according to the Laws of this Government. Given
under my hand in Hartford May ye 17th 1708.
in the Seaventh Year of her Majties Reign

G. Saltonstall.

No. 396.

to supply the vacancy so made, by power on them, according to the Laws of this Government. Given under my hand in Branford May ye 17th 1708.

in the Seaventh Year of her Majesties Reign

G. Saltonstall.

About a week since arrived a small Vessel at Salem from Guinea having had about six weeks passage from thence, what Intelligences he brings you will find in the inclosed Gazets and Letters which he to Coll. Hamilton may have the sight of after your perusal of. these Coll: Hamilton may have the sight of after your perusal of these

No other Vessel from Europe, parts have lately come after. No other Vessel from Europe, parts have lately come hither. I hope the next will be the Lord Bellomont with them. The French Army are busy this Ship from London, and every now and then forwarding about our Frontiers, and every now and then forwarding building

Som

London or other attending their Occasions in those parts notwith-
standing this partye that are constantly out ...... on that
.... and a body in a ready .... Service to the
.... not yet gained the Embargo .... Orders or ....
.... but at Newfound Land before .... as to ....
.... to go abroad all things without as to .... pray they not
.... in the best posture We can expect of, and pray they not
..... to make us ..... preparations: ....

Your ....
Affectionate humble Servant

Boston
August 9 1697

Wm Stoughton

I rec'd the favour of yours of the 26th of July past and of the 2?
of August current, with the Intelligence therein severally imparted
for which I return you Esq'r my hearty thanks
The success of Mons'r Bart against Carthagena will much annoy
the French flag his Master and be a very considerable supply for
his further fitting out the War of that plunder, get safe home
I am very sorry for the unhappy disappointment of Adm'r Neil
especially meeting with Bart's squadron:
I earnestly long to receive good Intelligence of this squadron
gone for Newfoundland. I have not heard anything from
or concerning them—

405   WARD, RICH'D, of Rhode Island. D. S. 4to. Feb. 23, 1726.

406   Ward, Rich'd. D. S. 4to. June 3, 1725.
> Petition to the General Assembly. Signed also by Nathaniel New-degate, D. Updike and Henry Bull.

407   Ward, Rich'd. D. S. Folio. March 14, 1726.

408   Winthrop, John, of Connecticut. Cut signature. " 1631." (Mounted).

409   Wright, James, of Georgia. D. S. Folio. Jan. 6, 1767.

410   Bull, Wm., of South Carolina. A. D. S. 4to. June 30, 1738, and cut signature.   2 pieces

411   Morris, Lewis, of New Jersey, and Chief Justice. A. D. S. Folio. Oct. 17, 1727.

412   Vaughan, Geo., of New Hampshire. A. D. S. Small 4to. May 8, 1718.

412a   Partridge, Wm., of New Hampshire. D. S. Folio. June 30, 1703.

412b   STOUGHTON, WM., OF MASSACHUSETTS. 1700. PRESIDING JUDGE AT THE TRIAL OF THE SALEM WITCHES. L. S. 4to. 2 pp. Boston, Aug. 9, 1697. To Gov. Fletcher of New York.
> Rare.

412c   Dudley, Jos., of Massachusetts. 1714. A. L. S. 4to. Boston, Sept. 14, 1705. With portrait.

412d   Ellis, Henry, of Georgia. D. S., 4to, Sept. 29, 1758; Jno. Reynolds, D. S., folio, July 6, 1756, and Henry Parker, cut signature.   3 pieces

412e   Hall, David, of Delaware. Col. in the Revolution. D. S. Folio. Lewes, June 17, 1776.

412f   Lyndon, Josias, of Rhode Island. D. S. (twice). 4to. Nov. 2, 1748.

412g   Fitch, Thos., of Connecticut. L. S. 4to. New Haven, Oct. 29, 1755.

GOVERNORS OF THE STATES.

413 Bibb, Thos., of Alabama. D. S. Folio. Nov. 9, 1820.

414 Bibb, Thos., of Alabama. A. L. S. 4to. Dec. 29, 1820.

415 Bibb, Wm. W., of Alabama. Two A. L's. S., 4tos. V. D.

416 Pickens, Israel, of Alabama. A. L. S. 4to. Aug. 17, 1822.

417 Moore, Gabriel, of Alabama. A. L. S. 4to. May 29, 1811.

418 Gayle, Jno., of Alabama. Two A. L's. S., 4tos., Nov. 14, 1835 and Sep. 21, 1832. 2 pieces

419 Collier, H. W., of Alabama. A. L. S. and two D's. S.
3 pieces

420 Yell, Archibald, of Arkansas. A. L. S. 8vo. March 8, 1846.

421 Treadwell, Jno., of Connecticut, and M. O. C. A. L. S. 4to. June 2, 1810.

422 Ellsworth, Wm. W., of Connecticut. Five A. L's. S., 4tos., and A. N S., in third person, 8vo. 6 pieces

423 Tomlinson, Gideon, of Connecticut. Two A. L's. S., folio and 4to. 2 pieces

424 Edwards, Henry W., of Connecticut. Two A. L's. S., 4to and folio. (Damaged). 2 pieces

425 Smith, Jno. Cotton, of Connecticut. Six A. L's. S., 4tos and folios, and A. D. S., folio. 7 pieces

426 Bissell, Clark, of Connecticut. Two A. L's. S., 4tos.
2 pieces.

427 Griswold, Roger, of Connecticut. A. L. S. Folio. Norwich, July 15, 1793.

428 Griswold, Matthew, of Connecticut. Three D's. S., folio and 4to. 3 pieces.

429 Trumbull, Joseph, of Connecticut. Three A. L's. S., 4tos.
3 pieces.

430 Foot, Sam'l A., of Connecticut. A. L. S., 4to and D. S., folio. 2 pieces.

431 Baldwin, Rogers S., of Connecticut. Two A. L's. S., 4tos.
2 pieces.

432 Dutton, Henry, of Connecticut. Three A. L's. S. 4to and 8vo. 3 pieces.

433 Miror, Wm. T., of Connecticut. A. L. S. 8vo. Oct. 27, 1866.

434 Andrews, Charles B., of Connecticut. A. L. S. 8vo. April 7, 1880.

435 Harrison, Henry B., of Connecticut. A. L. S. 4to. Nov. 27, 1879.

436 Haslet, Joseph, of Delaware. A. L. S. Folio. Dec. 25, 1816.

437 Folch, Vincenzo, of Florida. L. S. Folio. 1805.

438 Brown, Thomas, of Florida. L. S., 4to, and N. K. Call, L. S., 4to.   2 pieces.

439 McDuffie, Geo. of Georgia. A. L. S. 4to. April 22, 1845.

440 Milledge, John, of Georgia. A. L. S., 4to; Wilson Lump-kin, A. L. S., 4to; John Clark, L. S., 4to; Jno. Geddes, D. S., 4to; Wm. Rabun, two A. L's. S., 4tos. 6 pieces.

441 Troup, G. M., of Georgia. Five A. L's. S. 4tos. 5 pieces.

442 Gilmer, Geo. W. A. L. S. (initials), 4to and L. S., 4to ; J. Houstoun, A. D. S., folio ; Wm. C. Dawson, A. L. S., 4to and A. N. S., 8vo ; Wilson Lumpkin, D. S., and Wm. Schley, A. L. S., 4to.   7 pieces.

443 Martin, John, of Georgia. Two A. L's. S., 8vo and 4to, and A. L., folio; D. R. Mitchell, D. S., 4to, and Wilson Lumpkin, A. L. S., 4to.   5 pieces.

444 Johnson, Herschel V., of Georgia. Candidate for Vice-President. Six A. L's. S. 4tos.   6 pieces.

445 Jackson, James, of Georgia. Celebrated Officer in the Revolutionary War. A. L. S. 4to. 4 pp. Savannah, March 29, 1788.

446 Schley, Wm., of Georgia. A. L. S., 4to; D. B. Mitchell, A. L. S., 4to; J. M. Donald, A. L. S., 4to, and George Mathews, A. L. S., 4to.   4 pieces.

447 Reynold, John, of Illinois. Two A. L's. S., 4to, and D. S., 4to ; J. A. Matteson, D. S., 4to ; Wm. H. Bissell, A. L. S., 4to, and Thomas Ford, D. S., 4to.   6 pieces.

448 Edwards, Ninian, of Illinois. A. L. S. 4to. Vandalia, Dec. 11, 1830.

449 Jennings, Jonathan, of Indiana. A. L. S., 4to and L. S., 4to ; N. Noble, A. L. S., 4to and A. N. S., 4to ; Samuel Bigger, L. S., 4to, and James Whitcomb, D. S., 4to.
                                                        6 pieces.

450 Chambers, John, of Iowa. Two A. L's. S. 4tos. 2 pieces.

451 Dawson, John L., of Kansas. A. L. S. 4to. Aug. 15, 1864.

452 Morehead, J. T., of Kentucky. Four A. L's. S. 4tos.
                                                        4 pieces.

453 Clark, James, of Kentucky. A. L. S., 4to and D. S., 4to ; Wm. Ousley, A. L. S., 4to; C. S. Morehead, A. L. S., 4to, and Thomas Metcalf, two A. L's. S., 4tos. 6 pieces.

454 Metcalf, Thomas, of Kentucky. L. S., 4to ; L. W. Powell, A. L. S., 4to, and John L. Helm, D. S., folio. 3 pieces.

455 Claiborne, Wm. C. C., of Louisiana. Two A. L's. S. 4tos.
2 pieces.

456 Robertson, Thomas B., of Louisiana. A. L. S., 4to; Isaac
Johnson, A. L. S., 4to and D. S., 4to; A. B. Roman,
L. S., 4to; P. O. Herbert, A. L. S., 8vo; Jacques Vil-
lery, A. L. S., 4to, and P. Derbigny, A. L. S., 4to.
7 pieces.

457 Kent, Edward, of Maine. A. L. S. 4to. 4 pp. May 3,
1849.

458 Parris, Albion K., of Maine. Two A. L's. S., 4to and L. S.,
4to. 3 pieces.

459 Fairfield, John, of Maine. A. L. S., 4to; Samuel Wells,
A. L. S., 4to; W. G. Crosby, A. L. S., 8vo and D. S.,
4to; Enoch Lincoln, D. S., 4to. 5 pieces.

460 Lloyd, Edward, of Maryland. Three A. L's. S. 4to and
folio. 3 pieces.

461 Henry, John, of Maryland. A. L. S., 4to; C. Goldsborough, A. L. S., 4to and D. S., folio, and John Lee Carroll, A. L. S., 4to. 4 pieces.

462 Morton, Marcus, of Massachusetts. A. L. S. 4to. New
Bedford, March 10, 1835.

463 Phillips, Samuel. Lieut.-Governor of Massachusetts. Seven
A. L's. S. Folios and 4tos. 7 pieces.

464 Washburne, Emory, of Massachusetts. Two A. L's. S. 8vos.

465 Lincoln, Levi, of Massachusetts. Six A. L's. S. Folios and
4tos. 6 pieces.

466 Clifford, John H., of Massachusetts. A. L. S., 4to and
A. D. S., 4to. 2 pieces.

467 Sumner, Increase, of Massachusetts. D. S. 4to. June 1,
1777.

> State warrant. Beautifully engraved, and a fine specimen of the
> best work of Paul Revere.

468 Bowdoin, James, of Massachusetts. D. S. 4to. May 12,
1777.

> Treasury warrant. Signed by Caleb Cushing, Jabez Fisher, D.
> Sewall, S. Hilten, Benjamin Austin, H. Gardner and E. Thayer, Jr.

469 Gore, Chris. of Massachusetts. A. L. S. 4to. 2 pp.
Waltham, Oct. 6, 1820.

470 Woodbridge, Wm., of Michigan. A. L. S., 4to; G. B.
Porter, L. S., 4to, and Robert McClelland, A. L. S.,
8vo. 3 pieces.

471 Holmes, David, of Mississippi. A. L. S. 4to. Feb. 10,
1821.

472 Poindexter, George, of Mississippi. Three A. L's. S. 4tos.
3 pieces.

473 Brandon, Gerard C., of Mississippi. Five A. L's. S. 4tos.
5 pieces.

474 Scott, A. M., of Mississippi. Two D's. S., 4tos ; H. S. Foote, D. S., 4to ; John I. Guion, D. S., 4to. 4 pieces.

475 Brown, A. G., of Mississippi. A. L. S. 4to, and Nathaniel A. Ware, A. L. S., 4to. 2 pieces.

476 Hill, Isaac, of New Hampshire. A. L. S., 4to, and D. S., 4to. 2 pieces.

477 Plumer, Wm., of New Hampshire. Two A. L's. S., 4tos, A. N. S., 4to, and D. S., 4to. 4 pieces.

478 Plumer, Wm., of New Hampshire. Three A. L's. S. 4tos. 3 pieces.

479 Harvey, Matthew, of New Hampshire. A. L. S., 4to ; Samuel Bell, two A. L's. S., 4tos, and Henry Hubbard, A. L. S., 4to. 4 pieces.

480 Smith, Jeremiah, of New Hampshire. A. L. S. 4to. 4 pp. Philadelphia, April 6, 1792. To Josiah Bartlett.

480½ Harper, Joseph M., of New Hampshire. A. L. S. 4to. 2 pp. Dec. 23, 1833.

481 Smith, Jeremiah, of New Hampshire. Two A. L's. S. 4tos. 2 pieces.

482 Howell, Richard, of New Jersey. A. D. S. Folio. Trenton, June 10, 1795.

483 Dickerson, Philemon, of New Jersey. A. L. S. 4to. Feb. 4, 1841. With franked address.

484 Pennington, Wm. S., of New Jersey. A. L. S. Folio. Newark, March 3, 1821.

485 Howell, Richard, of New Jersey. A. L's. S., folio and 4to, and A. D. S., 4to. 3 pieces.

486 Bloomfield, Joseph, of New Jersey. A. L. S. 4to. Trenton, Oct. 26, 1807 ; and A. D. S., folio, 2 pp.

487 Vroom, Peter D., of New Jersey. Three A. L's. S., 4tos, and six A. L's. S., 8vos. 9 pieces.

488 Haines, Daniel, of New Jersey. A. L's. S. 4to. and 8vo. 2 pieces.

489 Parker, Joel, of New Jersey. A. L's. S. 4to. and 8vo. 2 pieces.

490 Pennington, Wm., of New Jersey. A. D. S., folio, 2 pp.; Chas. S. Olden, A. L. S., 8vo ; Mahlon Dickerson, A. L. S., 4to, and A. D., 4to. 4 pieces.

491 Throop, E. T., of New York. A. L. S. 4to. 9 pp. Albany, Dec. 4, 1831. To Wm. L. Marcy.
Political letter in reference to Martin Van Buren.

492 Throop, E. T., of New York. A. L. S. 4to. 9 pp.
Auburn, Aug. 15, 1865. To Francis Lieber.
Giving his views on the pardoning power of the Executive.

493 Throop, E. T., of New York. Five A. L's. S. 4tos.
5 pieces.

494 Wright, Silas, Jr., of New York. A. L. S. 4to. Washington, July 2, 1842.

495 Lewis, Morgan, of New York. A. L. S., 4to., June 12, 1811;
and A. L. S., 8vo., March 1, 1837.

496 Lewis, Morgan, of New York. A. L. S. 4to. March 11,
1807.
Relative to the purchase of 15.000 acres of land from the Oneida
Nation.

497 Yates, Jos. C., of New York. A. L. S., 4to; L. S., 4to, and
D. S., 4to. 3 pieces.

498 Hunt, Washington, of New York. Two A. L's. S., 8vos;
and Edwin D. Morgan, L. S, 8vo. 3 pieces

499 Stone, David, of North Carolina. A. L. S., 4to; James
Iredell, A. L. S., 4to; Chas. Manly, A. L. S., 8vo;
David L. Swain, L. S., 4to. 4 pieces.

500 Miller, Wm., of North Carolina. A. L. S., folio; John
Owen, A. L. S., 8vo; John Branch, L. S., 4to, and
Patrick Noble, signature. 4 pieces.

501 Shunk, Francis R., of Pennsylvania. Five A. L's. S., 4tos;
and D. S., 4to. 6 pieces.

502 Bigler, Wm., of Pennsylvania. D. S., 4to., and David R.
Porter, A. L. S., 8vo. 2 pieces.

503 Huntington, Sam'l., of Ohio. Seven A. L's. S., folios and
4tos. 7 pieces.
A series of long and interesting letters.

504 Shannon, Wilson, of Ohio. Two A. L's. S., 4tos. 2 pieces.

505 Byrd, C. W. Acting Governor of Ohio. A. L. S., 4to,
2 pp., and A. L. S., folio. 2 pieces.

506 Looker, Othniel, of Ohio. A. L. S., 4to; Allen Trimble,
A. L. S., 4to; Ethan A. Brown, A. L. S., 4to, and
Wm. Allen, A. L. S., 8vo. 4 pieces.

507 Bartley, T. W., of Ohio. Three A. L's. S., 8vos; Seabury
Ford, L. S., 4to, and D. S., 4to. 5 pieces.

508 Francis, J. B., of Rhode Island. A. L. S., 4to; Wm. B.
Lawrence, two A. L's. S., 8vos; F. M. Dimond, D. S., 4to;
Byron Diman, D. S., 4to; Arthur Fenner, A. D. S., 4to;
James Y. Smith, signature; Jabez Bowen, Lieut.-Gov.,
four A. L's. S., 4tos and folios. 11 pieces.

509 Hayne, Robert Y., of South Carolina. A. L. S. 4to. 3 pp. Washington, Jan. 28, 1825.

510 Drayton, Jno., of South Carolina. Six A. L's. S., 4tos and folios. 6 pieces.
Long and interesting letters on public affairs.

511 Johnson, David, of South Carolina. A. L. S., 4to; Jno. L. Wilson, A. L. S. and A. D. S., 4tos; J. Hamilton, A. L. S., 4to; B. K. Hennegan, A. L. S., 4to; Thos. Pinckney, D. S., and Benj. Guerard, A. L. S., 4to (third person). 7 pieces.

512 Henderson, J. P., of Texas. Three A. L's. S., 4to and 8vo. 3 pieces.

513 Tyler, John, of Virginia. A. L. S. 4to. Richmond, May 11, 1810.

514 Tyler John, of Virginia. D. S. 4to. With seal. Richmond, May 11, 1810.

515 Tyler, John, of Virginia. A. L. S. 4to. 3 pp. Charles City, April 17, 1782.

516 Giles, Wm. B., of Virginia. A. L. S., 4to, and L. S., 4to; L. W. Tazewell, A. L. S., 4to; Wm. H. Cabell, L. S., 4to; James Pleasants, A. L. S., 4to, and L. S., 4to; John Letcher, A. L. S., 4to, and Robert Brooke, A. L. S., 4to. 8 pieces.

517 Wise, Henry A., of Virginia. Hung John Brown. A. L. S. 4to. Accomac, June 16, 1843.

518 Jenison, S. H., of Vermont. D. S., folio; Stephen Royce, D. S., folio, and Jno. S. Robinson, D. S., folio. 3 pieces.

519 Tichener, Isaac, of Vermont. Five A. L's. S., folios, and two A. L's. S., 4tos. 7 pieces.

520 Crafts, Sam'l C., of Vermont. Three A. L's. S. 4tos. 3 pieces.

521 Mattocks, John, of Vermont. A. L. S., 4to; Hiland Hall, A. L. S.; Jonas Galusha, A. L. S., 4to, and D. S., 4to: J. Gregory Smith, A. L. S., 8vo. 5 pieces.

522 Skinner, Rich'd, of Vermont. Three A. L's. S. 4tos. 3 pieces.

523 Van Ness, C. P., of Vermont. Three A. L's. S. 4tos. 3 pieces.

524 Boreman, A. J., of West Virginia. A. L. S. 4to. Feb. 18, 1879.

525 Doty, James D., of Wisconsin. A. L. S. 4to. Jan. 24, 1856.

COLONIAL.

526 **A**DDINGTON, ISAAC. Chief Justice of Massachusetts, 1702. D. S. 4to. Nov. 17, 1703. Signed also by Samuel Converse.

527 Addington, Isaac. A. D. S. 4to. Jan. 28, 1679. (Damaged).

528 Alexander, James. Att'y-Gen'l of New York. Father of Lord Stirling. A. L. S., 4to, New York, December 13, 1752, and A. L. S., folio, 2 pp., New York, Feb. 19, 1721.

529 Amory, Thos. Distinguished Boston Merchant. A. D. S. 4to. Portsmouth, Aug. 21, 1719.

530 Atkinson, Theodore. Colonial Chief Justice of New Hampshire. Three A. D's. S., folios. 1703, 1710 and 1711. 3 pieces.

531 Atkinson, Theodore. Albany Convention of 1754. L. S., folio, Portsmouth, April 7, 1773, and A. D. S., folio, May 13, 1748. 2 pieces.

532 **B**OWLER, METCALF. Member of the Congress of 1765. A. D. Folio. 2 pp.
    Essay on generosity and hospitality.

533 Bradley, Richard. · Attorney-General of New York. D. S. Folio. May 4, 1743.

534 Brooke, Francis. Officer in the Revolutionary War. Virginia Judge. A. L. S. 4to. 4 pp. St. Julian, Jan. 22, 1828.

535 Brooke, Francis. A. L. S. 4to. 3 pp. Richmond, Jan. 13, 1828. To Jas. Monroe.

536 Byfield, Nathaniel. Speaker of the Massachusetts House of Representatives. A. D. S. 8vo. 1704.
    One of the four proprietors of the town of Bristol, Rhode Island. Wrote an account of the overthrow of Andros.

537 Byfield, Nathaniel. A. L. S. Folio. 2 pp. Bristol, Aug. 28, 1718. To Rev. Thos. Prince, and indorsed in Prince's handwriting.

538 **C**HAMBERS, JOHN. Albany Convention of 1754. D. S. Folio. July 24, 1750.

539 Chandler, John. Albany Convention of 1754. A. L. S. 4to. Roxbury, June 15, 1714.

540 Checkley, Anthony. First Attorney-General of Massachusetts, under the Charter of 1691. A. D. S. Folio. 2 pp. Sep. 12, 1699.

1710 Comm of Boston Dr to Josiah ffranklin
by Cand & do to Battery

May	9	to 2ᵉ Candles — —	00	01	03
	19	to 3ᵉ ditto — — —	00	02	00
Jun	8	to 2ᵉ ditto — — —	00	01	04
	18	to 3ᵉ ditto — — —	00	02	00
July	4	to 5 ditto — — —	00	03	04
aug	12	to 5ˢ ditto — —	00	03	04
Sep	9	to 2 ditto — — —	00	01	04
	22	to ½ Doz ditto — —	00	04	00
oct	29	to ½ Doz ditto —	00	04	00
no	22	to ½ Doz ditto —	00	04	00
Dec	26	to 2ᵉ ditto —	00	01	04
Jan	1	to 4ᵉ ditto — —	00	02	08
	24	to ½ Doz ditto —	00	04	00
feb	24	to ½ Doz ditto — —	00	04	00
mar	2	to 5ᵉ ditto —	00	03	04
may	1	to 5ᵉ ditto —	00	03	04
Jun	26	to 1ᵉ ditto —	00	00	08
July	9	to 2ᵉ ditto —	00	01	04
	21	to 2ˢ ditto —	00	02	00
aug	5	to 3ˢ ditto —	00	03	04
	28	to ½ Doz ditto —	00	04	00
Sep	25	to 3ᵉ ditto —	00	02	00
no	27	to 3ᵉ ditto —	00	02	00
Dec	19	to 3ᵉ ditto —	00	04	00
	30	to ½ Doz ditto —	00	04	00
feb	1	to ½ Doz ditto —	00	04	00

£ 03 | 11 | 11

No. 332.

541   Cooper, Wm. New York Judge and Revolutionary Patriot. Father of J. Fenimore Cooper. A. L. S. Folio. 3 pp. Cooperstown, Dec. 17, 1794.

542   Cooper, Wm. Five A. L's. S., folios and 4tos. Various dates.   5 pieces.

543   Cooper, Wm. Two A. D's. S., folios. Various dates.
                                           2 pieces.

544   DAVENPORT, ADDINGTON. Colonial Justice Supreme Court of Massachusetts. D. S. 4to. Dec. 3, 1704. Signed also by Paul Dudley, Chief Justice of Massachusetts.

545   Delaware. Recommendation to Cæsar Rodney, President of Delaware, appointing certain men as Receivers of Supplies for the Continental Army, dated May 2, 1780. Signed by all the Justices of the Court of Quarter Sessions for the Counties of Sussex and Lewes. Folio.

546   Dudley, Paul. Colonial Att'y-Gen. of Massachusetts. D. S. Folio. Aug. 4, 1712.

547   Dwight, Timothy. Colonial Judge of Massachusetts. A. D. S. Folio. Nov. 13, 1753.

548   De Lancy, James. Albany Convention of 1754. Parchment D. S., 4to, and D. S., folio, by Elizabeth De Lancy, Oct. 15, 1775. Signed also by J. Watts, Recorder.
                                           2 pieces.

549   De Peyster, Abraham. Colonial Governor of Maryland. A. D. S. 4to.

     Signed as Chairman of the Committee to whom a bill entitled " An Act for Reviving An Act for Regulating Slaves," was committed.

550   FARRAR, TIMOTHY. Revolutionary Officer; Chief Justice of New Hampshire. A. L. S. 4to. 2 pp. April, 1821.

551   Faneuil, Peter. After whom Faneuil Hall was named. D. S. Folio. 2 pp. May 22, 1732.

552   Franklin, Josiah. Father of Benjamin Franklin. A. D. S. (with signature in the body). 8vo. 1710.

     Very rare.

553   Freeman, Samuel. Revolutionary Patriot. Folio. Portland, March 31, 1805.

554   Frisbie, Levi. Missionary to the Indians. A. L. S. 4to. Ipswich, Dec. 30, 1775.

555   GORDON, THOS. Colonial Chief Justice of New Jersey. A. D. S. 4to. Amboy, 1703.

556   Gordon, Thos. Knox. Chief Justice of South Carolina. 2 D's. S. Folios. 1774.   2 pieces.

557   Graham, Jas. Speaker of the House of Representatives of New York and first Recorder of New York city. A. D. S. 4to. April 21, 1691.

558   Greene, Wm. Patriotic Governor of Rhode Island during the Revolutionary War. A. L. S. 4to. Warwick, Aug. 19, 1780.

559   Gridley, Jeremiah. Att'y-Gen'l of Massachusetts under the Province Charter. A. D. S. 4 pp. 4to. Aug., 1755.
    Fine specimen.

560   HALL, KINSLEY. Provincial Counsellor of New Hampshire. D. S. Folio. 2 pp. November 13, 1696. Signed also by Henry Lowe, Jno. Woodman, John Tuttle, Thomas Atkinson and Wm. Bedford.

561   Hall, Elihu. Judge of Connecticut. A. L. S. 4to. New Haven, Jan. 10, 1769.
    Refers to Benedict Arnold.

562   Hamilton, Alex. General in the Revolution and Aide to Washington. D. S. Folio. 3 pp. Albany, Jan. 29, 1800.

563   Hamilton, John. Colonial Governor of New Jersey. A. L. S. 4to. 3 pp. Amboy, Oct. 17, 1719.

564   HATHORNE, JOSEPH. **One of the Massachusetts Witch Judges.** A. D. S. 4to. Signed three times. Salem, Sept. 29, 1684.
    Fine specimen and rare.

565   Hinckes, John. First Chief Justice of New Hampshire. President of Council. A. D. S. 4to. March 16, 1703.

566   Hepworth, George. Colonial Chief Justice of South Carolina. D. S. 4to. August 13, 1725.

567   Horsmanden, Daniel. Author of the "History of the Negro Plot in New York." Chief Justice, and Commissioner to Inquire into the Burning of the "Gaspé." A. L. S. Folio. 2 pp. New York, Nov. 28, 1734. To Gov. Colden.

568   Horsmanden, Daniel. D. S. Small 4to. No date.

569   Huger, Jos. Member of the Old Congress. Signature on a piece of South Carolina Continental paper money, dated 1776. Signed also by Jacob Motte and Alex. Moultrie.

570   Huske, Ellis. Colonial Postmaster of Boston. Published the *Boston Weekly Post-Boy.* D. S. 4to. 2 pp. Portsmouth, March 6, 1741.

571   Hutchinson, Thomas. Colonial Governor of Massachusetts and Member of the Albany Convention of 1754. A. L. S. 8vo. Boston, May 3, 1757.

Lot 564 should read John Hathorne, not Joseph Hathorne.

557 Graham, Jas. Speaker of the House of Representatives of New York and first Recorder of New York city. A. D. S. 4to. April 21, 1691.

558 Greene, Wm. Patriotic Governor of Rhode Island during the Revolutionary War. A. L. S. 4to. Warwick, Aug. 19, 1780.

559 Gridley, Jeremiah. Att'y-Gen'l of Massachusetts under the Province Charter. A. D. S. 4 pp. 4to. Aug., 1755. Fine specimen.

560 HALL, KINSLEY. Provincial Counsellor of New Hampshire. D. S. Folio. 2 pp. November 13, 1696. Signed also by Henry Lowe, Jno. Woodman, John Tuttle, Thomas Atkinson and Wm. Bedford.

President of Council. A. D. S. 4to. March 10, 1703.

566 Hepworth, George. Colonial Chief Justice of South Carolina. D. S. 4to. August 13, 1725.

567 Horsmanden, Daniel. Author of the "History of the Negro Plot in New York." Chief Justice, and Commissioner to Inquire into the Burning of the "Gaspé." A. L. S. Folio. 2 pp. New York, Nov. 28, 1734. To Gov. Colden.

568 Horsmanden, Daniel. D. S. Small 4to. No date.

569 Huger, Jos. Member of the Old Congress. Signature on a piece of South Carolina Continental paper money, dated 1776. Signed also by Jacob Motte and Alex. Moultrie.

570 Huske, Ellis. Colonial Postmaster of Boston. Published the *Boston Weekly Post-Boy.* D. S. 4to. 2 pp. Portsmouth, March 6, 1741.

571 Hutchinson, Thomas. Colonial Governor of Massachusetts and Member of the Albany Convention of 1754. A. L. S. 8vo. Boston, May 3, 1757.

Sarah Joe testifieth that she last Saturday was fortnight George
Harris of Marblehead who then liued in the house of Elizabeth
Risbee was deuouring in the about house with Mary Ricketts
and shee talking of him yet shee sayd bee must beare some money
I heard bee sayd George Harris ownes that bee had put away his
money in taking of a shop & buying of papers .

Sworne before John Hathorne Assist
Salem Sepr 24th 1694 —

Eliz abeth Risbee testifieth that the last Saturday was fortnight
George Harris of Marblehead who liued in my house was deuouring
with Mary Ricketts & in his discourse bee told her bee must borrow
his marrying before bee bought a quarter of meate of
some money and that hea had borough Bue liue the
his landlord But bee had not money to pay him for it Bue sayd
bee should shee next worke :

Sworne before John Hathorne Assist

557 Graham, Jas. Speaker of the House of Representatives of New York and first Recorder of New York city. A. D. S. 4to. April 21, 1691.

558 Greene, Wm. Patriotic Governor of Rhode Island during the Revolutionary War. A. L. S. 4to. Warwick, Aug. 19, 1780.

559 Gridley, Jeremiah. Att'y-Gen'l of Massachusetts under the Province Charter. A. D. S. 4 pp. 4to. Aug., 1755. Fine specimen.

560 HALL, KINSLEY. Provincial Counsellor of New Hampshire. D. S. Folio. 2 pp. November 13, 1696. Signed also by Henry Lowe, Jno. Woodman, John Tuttle, Thomas Atkinson and Wm. Bedford.

President of Council. A. D. S. 4to. March 10, 1703.

566 Hepworth, George. Colonial Chief Justice of South Carolina. D. S. 4to. August 13, 1725.

567 Horsmanden, Daniel. Author of the "History of the Negro Plot in New York." Chief Justice, and Commissioner to Inquire into the Burning of the "Gaspé." A. L. S. Folio. 2 pp. New York, Nov. 28, 1734. To Gov. Colden.

568 Horsmanden, Daniel. D. S. Small 4to. No date.

569 Huger, Jos. Member of the Old Congress. Signature on a piece of South Carolina Continental paper money, dated 1776. Signed also by Jacob Motte and Alex. Moultrie.

570 Huske, Ellis. Colonial Postmaster of Boston. Published the *Boston Weekly Post-Boy.* D. S. 4to. 2 pp. Portsmouth, March 6, 1741.

571 Hutchinson, Thomas. Colonial Governor of Massachusetts and Member of the Albany Convention of 1754. A. L. S. 8vo. Boston, May 3, 1757.

Salem Sept 29 1694

The testimony of William Furnies who sayth that one day this
fortnight George Harris of Marblehead with Goe: in the hering of
Elizabeth Russell came along befor my gate & told me that a
him his poner to God him did Goe: & if hee would give me a
for poule for charge & would pay him. goe: hes put his hand by
his syde & as I suppose into that purses & puled out money
not only once but to my Ber remembrance then put it in a
forond byme in like manner & Goe: goues after porner. &
payd him & furtther sayth not —

Sworn before me: John Hathorne Assist
Salem Sept: 29 1694 —

No. 564.

572 Hutchinson, Thomas. A. L. 4to. Boston, Oct. 18, 1757. To Lord Loudoun.

573 Hutchinson, Thomas. D. S. Folio. Boston, Nov. 20, 1761.

574 IRVINE, JAMES. Served under Bouquet. Brigadier-General in the Rev. War. Two D's. S. 4tos. 1785.

575 JAFFREY, GEORGE. Chief Justice of New Hamshire. A. L. S. Folio. Portsmouth, July, 31, 1784, and D. S., folio, Aug. 27, 1719.

576 Johnson, Wm. Samuel. Signer of the Constitution. L. S. 4to. 2 pp. Stratford, April 3, 1802.

577 Jones, David. Colonial Judge of the Supreme Court of New York. D. S. Folio. April 6, 1736.

578 Jones, Samuel. Member of the Old Congress. A. L. S. 4to. New York, May 11, 1797.

579 Jones, Samuel. A. D. S., folio, 9 pp.; and three D's. S., folios. No dates. 4 pieces.

580 KIRBY, EPHRAIM. Served in the Battle of Bunker Hill. A. L. S. 4to. Litchfield, Sept. 29, 1798.

581 Kollock, S. Officer in the Revolutionary War. A. D. S. Small 4to. Dec. 17, 1787.

582 LEEDS, DANIEL. Almanac Maker and Colonial Judge. A. D. S. 4to. 2 pp. Burlington, March, 1696.

583 Livingston, Robt. R. Member of the Congress of 1765 and of the Old Congress. Administered the oath to Washington. A. L. S. Folio. 2 pp. Oct. 19, 1775.

584 Livingston, Robt. R. A. L. S. Folio. New York, May 25, 1766.

585 Ludlow, Geo. D. Tory Supreme Court Judge of New York. A. L. S. 4to. July 30, 1776.

586 Lusk, Stephen. Lieut.-Col. in the Revolution. A. L. S. 4to. 2 pp. Feb. 22, 1786.

587 MATHEWS, JNO. Member of the Old Congress. Signature on a portion of a Continental note. Also signed by Jacob Motte and Thos. Savage.

588 Morton, Perez. Patriot. Delivered the oration on General Warren, in 1776. Four A. L's. S., folios and 4tos. Various dates. 4 pieces.

589 Murray, Jos. Albany Convention of 1754. A. D. S. Small 4to. Feb. 3, 1725.

590 McLene, James. Member of the Old Congress. A. D. S. 4to. Jan. 2, 1778.

591 NEW YORK. Early Document relating to lands in the Mohawk country, in New York. Dated Oct., 1723. Signed by Abraham Wendell, Lewis Morris, Jr. and others.

592 New York. Early Document relating to vacant lands within the Province of New York. Dated Nov., 1766. Signed by Robert Morris, Sam'l Huntington, Jno. Longworth and others.

593 Nicholas, Rob't Carter. Revolutionary Patriot, of Virginia. A. L. S. 4to. July 23, 1779.

594 OLIVER, ANDREW. Stamp Act Commissioner and Lieutenant-Governor of Massachusetts. A. L. S. 4to. Boston, Sept. 8, 1768.

595 Oliver, Andrew. Part of A. L. S. 4to. Boston, Sept. 20, 1768.

596 Ogle, Sam'l. Colonial Governor of Maryland. L. S. Folio.

597 Otis, James. Member of Stamp Act Congress and Distinguished Revolutionary Patriot. A. D. S. 4to. March, 1767.
Very rare.

598 Otis, Sam'l A. Member of the Old Congress. A. L. S. 4to. 2 pp. New York, Nov. 29, 1787. With franked address. Signed also by Geo. Thatcher, Member of the Old Congress.

599 PALMER, JNO. Colonial Military Officer and Judge of New York. D. S. Folio. Aug. 6, 1684.

600 Philips, Adolph. Colonial Judge of New York. Parchment D. S. 4to. No date.

601 Pickering, John. Member of the Constitutional Convention. A. L. S. 4to. Portsmouth, June 30, 1796.

602 Pinckney, Chas. Colonial Chief Justice of South Carolina. A. L. S., 4to, 1765, and three D's. S., 4tos. Various dates. 4 pieces.

603 Putnam, J. Officer in the French and Indian War. A. L. S. 4to. Worcester, Dec. 15, 1753.

604 Pynchon, John. Principal Military and Civil Officer in Hampshire Co. A. L. S. Folio. Boston, May 18, 1672.
An affectionate letter to his son, Joseph.

605 RANDOLPH, EDWARD. First Attorney-General of New Hampshire. A. D. S. Folio. Nov. 27, 1686.

606 Read, Chas. Officer in the Revolution. Made his submission to the British. A. L. S. 4to. June 28, 1761.

607 Ridgely, Nicholas. Colonial Supreme Court Judge of Delaware. D. S. Folio. Aug. 19, 1746.

608 Riker, R. Recorder of New York. A. L. S. Folio. New York, Aug. 26, 1806.

    The hero of Halleck's poem, "The Recorder."

609 S̲ALTONSTALL, NATHANIEL. **A Member of the Special Court Appointed for the Trial of the Salem Witches.** A. L. S. Folio. Haverhill, July 7, 1765. Addressed to Governor John Leverett and indorsed in the Governor's handwriting.

    Very rare.

610 SALTONSTALL, RICH'D. Colonial Judge of Massachusetts. A. L. S. 4to. Boston, April 1, 1746.

611 SEWALL, SAMUEL. **One of the Seven Judges Appointed for the Trial of the Salem Witches.** A. L. S. Folio. 2 pp. Boston, Dec. 2, 1698. To Rev. Nehemiah Hobart, at Newton.

    We quote a few extracts from this very rare letter :—

    He refers to "The Dismal Persecution of the Brethren of our Jesus in France, having first seen it to-day, Our Comfort is they are HIS, and HE will Magnificently Save them from their Sins and Enemys, Hath Lewis yᵉ 14th an arm like God, or can he Thunder with a Voice like HIM?" * * * * "Mr Noyes Brought over a Book lately set forth by a Friar, giving an accᵒ of his Discoveries in America on yᵉ backside of yᵉ Province, and of his Opinion that America is joined with Asia, and that there are no such Straits as the Straits Anian, The Country is larger than Europe, peopled with many nations of Indians, Name of yᵉ Author is Hanapin, as I take it, he went from Canada, Dedicates his book to K. William. I have not yet got sight of it." Etc.

612 SEWALL, SAMUEL. A. L. S. Folio. Boston, Dec. 5, 1727.

613 SEWALL, SAMUEL. A. L. S. Folio. Boston, July 12, 1692. To John Walley. With Address.

614 SEWALL, SAMUEL, Autograph Paraphrase of Isaiah, Chapter XXVI. Folio. 3 pp. Oct. 3, 1698.

    We quote the first verse :—

> "A city strong for us there is,
> Salvation makes the fort and wall.
> Set open ye the gates, and then
> The righteous nation enter shall,
> Preserving truths, the firm decree
> Peacefull and bless'd prosperitie
> Shall well secure to him forever
> Because he puts his trust in thee."

615 SEWALL, SAMUEL. Autograph Notes in Latin and Greek. 4to. 10 pp.

616 SEWALL, SAMUEL. Autograph Notes of Sermons. 8vo.
32 pp. (Somewhat damaged).

> We quote from the "Memorial History of Boston":—"In 1697, Jan.
> 14th, Judge Sewall handed to the Minister of the South Church his
> memorable confession of his part in these mournful transactions [trial
> of the witches] and stood to hear it read, bowing when it was finished.
> There is a common tradition, that on one day of every year, to the end
> of his long life, the good man and Magistrate kept a day of private
> prayer and humiliation in acknowledgment of his guilt, and in supli-
> cation for mercy." * * * * "Judge Sewall is the Pepys of New
> England. His diary is as quaint and racy, and as full of delicious bits
> of self-revealing as that of his English contemporary."

617 Sewall, Stephen. Colonial Judge of Massachusetts. Son
of Samuel Sewall. A. D. S. 4to. Salem, May 4, 1678.

618 Sewall, Samuel. The Younger. Colonial Judge of Massachusetts. A. D. S. 4to. Sept. 11, 1790.

619 Sherburne, Henry. Albany Convention of 1754. Chief
Justice of New Hampshire. A. L. S. 4to. Ports-
mouth, Nov. 3, 1758.
Rare.

620 Sherburne, Henry. Four D's. S. 4tos. Various dates.
4 pieces.

621 Smith, Wm. Albany Convention of 1754. D. S. Folio.
3 pp. Oct. 15, 1765.

622 TROTT, NICHOLAS. Colonial Chief Justice of South
Carolina. Three D's. S. Folios. Various dates.
3 pieces.

623 Troup, Robert. Colonel in the Revolution, Aide to Arnold
and Treasurer of the Continental Congress. A. L. S.
4to. 3 pp. April 1, 1809.

624 Troup, Robert. A. L. S. Folio. July 13, 1779.

625 Trowbridge, Edmund. Attorney-General of Massachusetts
under the Province Charter. A. D. S., folio, July 20,
1762, and A. D. S., small 4to, July 30, 1753.

626 Townsend, C. Chancellor of the Exchequer, and promotor
of the Stamp Act. D. S. Folio. May 10, 1770.
Signed also by C. Jenkinson, first Earl of Liverpool
and Secretary of War under Lord North, 1778.

627 Turner, Geo. Revolutionary Officer; highly distinguished
in the southern campaign. Judge of the N. W. Territory. A. L. S. Folio. 2 pp. Fort Washington, Sept.
1, 1790.

628 Turner, Geo. A. D. S. 4to. Oct. 29, 1802.

629 Tucker, Samuel. President of the Committee of Safety.
A. L. S. Folio. Trenton, Sept. 15, 1783.

630 UPHAM, JOSHUA. Tory Chief Justice of St. John. A. L. S. Small 4to. June 29, 1772.

631 VAN SCHAACK, PETER. Bitter partisan and pronounced Tory. A. L. S. 4to. 2 pp. No date.

632 Van Vechten, Abraham. Patriarch of the New York Bar. A. L. S. Folio. Aug. 31, 1810.

633 Varick, Richard. Aide to Washington. L. S. 4to. New York, Jan. 1, 1829.

634 Vaughan, Wm. Chief Justice of New Hampshire. A. D. S., folio, Salesbury, Jan. 4, 1706, and D. S., 4to, April 4, 1675.

635 WALDRON, RICHARD. Colonial Secretary of New Hampshire. A. L. S. 4to. May 28, 1738.

636 Ward, Samuel. Colonel in the Revolution. Member of the Hartford Convention. A. L. S. 4to. New York, Sept. 14, 1785.

637 Weare, Meshech. Albany Convention of 1754. President of N. H. in 1776 A. D. S., 4to, Exeter, July 6, 1782, and D. S., small 4to, March 24, 1781. 2 pieces.

638 Wiggin, Andrew. Colonial Judge of New Hamphire. A. D. S. 4to. Jan. 29, 1700. (Damaged).

639 Wingate, Paine. Member of the Old Congress. Signature on folio sheet.

640 Worthington, John. Albany Convention of 1754. A. D. S. 4to. May 24, 1754.

641 Worthington, J. Stamp Act Congress. A. L. S. 4to. Springfield, Jan. 9, 1798.

642 YATES, ROBERT. Member of the Constitutional Convention. D. S. Folio. 1782.

643 South Carolina Documents. Signed by the Colonial Chief Justices and Judges:—Nicholas Trott, 1703; Robt. Gibbes, 1708; Robt. Daniell, 1714; Chas. Hill, 1722; Rich'd Allein, 1730; Benj. Whitaker, 1739–1746; Robt. Austin, 1739; James Graeme, 1749; Peter Leigh, 1757; James Mickie, 1760; Robt. Pringle, 1760; Thos. Knox Gordon, 1774; Henry Pendleton, 1786, and E. M. Ray, 1791. Folios. 16 pieces.

644 Wiggin, Andrew. Colonial Judge of New Hampshire. D. S., 4to, 1726, and D. S:, 4to, of Shadrach Walton, 1706; Jno. Plaisted, 1706; Geo. Jaffrey, 1720; Thos. Atkinson, 1675; Francis Noal, 1670, and Elias Hildman, 1676; all of whom were Colonial Judges of New Hampshire. 7 pieces.

645 Old Parchment Document, dated 1785, with two rare, blue, English revenue stamps.

646 Old Parchment Document, dated 1705, with rare, blue, English revenue stamp.

647 Old Parchment Document, dated 1701, with two rare, blue, English revenue stamps.

648 Delaware. Letters and Documents relating to the State of Delaware in Colonial and Revolutionary Times. Good lot. 50 pieces.

AUTHORS.

649 ALEXANDER, J. H. Scientist. A. L. S. 8vo. Phila., Jan. 11, 1851.

650 Allibone, S. Austin. Author of " Dictionary of English Literature." A. L. S. 8vo. 4 pp. Philada., Oct. 20, 1854.

651 Angell, Joseph K. Distinguished legal writer. A. L. S., in the third person. 4to. Sept. 13, 1840.

652 Anthon, Wm. Author. A. L. S. 4to. New York, Feb. 15, 1840.

653 Arnold, J. V. Author of " Life of Lincoln." A. L. S. 8vo. Washington, Feb. 24, 1864.

654 Austin, James T. Author of " Life of Elbridge Gerry. A. L. S. 4to. Boston, May 1, 1841.

655 BACHMAN, JOHN. American naturalist. Assisted Audubon in his great work on ornithology. A. L. S. 4to. May 15, 1843.

656 Beecher, Henry Ward. Eminent preacher and author. A. L. S. 8vo. 2 pp. Brooklyn, June 2, 1866.

657 Bethune, Geo. W. Eminent divine, poet and scholar. A. L. S. 8vo. Brooklyn, July 11, 1857.

658 Bigelow, John. Author, and editor of the *New York Evening Post*. A. L. S. 4to. 2 pp. April 24, 1849.

659 Bird, Robert M. Author of " The Gladiator." A. L. S. 4to. Dec. 31, 1847.

660 Bishop, Abraham. Political writer. A. L. S. 4to. New Haven, March 23, 1803.

661 Bishop, R. P. Poet. A. L. S. 8vo. 2 pp. Auburn, Oct. 26, 1803.

662 Blackwell, Elizabeth. First woman that ever received the degree of M. D. in the United States. A. L. S. 8vo. Paris, Sept. 25, 1849.

663 Blake, John L. American biographer. A. L. S. 4to. Boston, Dec. 15, 1825.

664 Blunt, Joseph. Author. A. L. S. 4to. New York, April 17, 1835.

665 Boker, Geo. H. American poet. A. L. S. 8vo. No date.

666 Brackenridge, Henry M. American judge and writer; published " A History of the Second War With Great Britain." A. L. S. Folio. 3 pp. Pensacola, Dec. 26, 1821.

667 Brackenridge, Henry M. A. L. S. 4to. Harrisburg, Feb. 12, 1846.

668 Briggs, Chas. F. Author and editor. A. L. S. 8vo. 4 pp. New York. No date.

669 Bryant, Wm. Cullen. Distinguished poet. A. L. S. 8vo. New York, June 26, 1848.

670 Buckingham, Joseph T. American journalist. A. L. S. 4to. Louisville, June 6, 1840.

671 CAREY, HENRY C. Political economist. Two A. L's. S., 8vos. No date.

672 Chester, Anson G. A. L. S. 4to. Albany, Oct. 30 1863.

673 Childs, Casper C. Editor of *The Jeffersonian.* A. L. S. 4to. New York, May 8, 1838.

674 Combe, Geo. Eminent phrenologist. A. L. S. 8vo. 2 pp. March 1, 1839.

675 Comte Auguste. French philospher. Founder of *" Positivisme."* A. L. S. Small 8vo. 3 pp. Paris, Dec. 1, 1854.

676 Conkling, F. A. Political writer. A. L. S. 4to. New York, Oct. 16, 1849.

677 Cooper, Thomas. Natural philosopher and lawyer; president of the University of South Carolina. A. L. S. 4to. Dec. 10, 1838.

678 Conrad, Rob't T. Author, and Mayor of Philadelphia. Two D's. S., 4tos. 2 pieces.

679 Córdova, A. de. Author and lecturer. A. L. S. 8vo. 2 pp. Oct. 27, 1865.

680 Crafts, Wm. Poet. A. L. S. 4to. Charleston, Dec. 18, 1798.

681 Curtis, Geo. Ticknor. Eminent legal writer. A. L. S. 8vo. Boston. No date.

682 DANA, CHARLES A. Journalist. A. L. S. 8vo. New York, Feb. 18. No date.

683 Davis, Matthew L. Author of the " Life of Aaron Burr." A. L. S. 4to. New York, November 20, 1839.

684 De Bow, Jas. D. B. American writer and statistician. A.
L. S. 8vo. New York, May 13, 1854.

685 Doane, Geo. W. American poet and ecclesiastic. A. L.
S. 8vo. 3 pp. No date.

686 Dickens, Chas. Eminent English novelist. Franked addressed envelope.

687 Dillon, John F. Legal author. A. L. S. 8vo. May
23. No year.

688 Drake, Benj. Author. Editor of *The Cincinnati Chroni-
cle*. A. L. S. 8vo. 2 pp. No date.

689 Drinker, Anna ("Edith May"). American poetess. A. L.
S. 8vo. No date.

690 Dulany, Daniel. Celebrated lawyer, writer and Revolutionary patriot. A. L. S., 4to, Baltimore, May 13, 1785,
and A. D. S., 4to, Oct. 12, 1772. 2 pieces.

691 E LDER, WM. Author. A. L. S. 8vo. 2 pp. July
15, 1853.

692 Elliot, Jonathan. Editor of "Debates on the Constitutional
Convention of 1787." A. L. S. 4to. 2 pp. Washington, Oct. 7, 1829.

693 Everett, Edward. Distinguished American orator, statesman and scholar. A. L. S. 4to. Boston, Dec. 10, 1851.

694 F ORESTER, FANNY. American author. Autograph
poem, signed. 8vo. Philadelphia, Feb. 2, 1846.

695 G REELEY, HORACE. Distinguished American journalist. A. L. S. 4to. New York, April 26, 1851.

696 Green, Duff. American editor. Two A. L's. S., 4tos,
Washington, March 19, 1866, and Philadelphia, Nov.
7, 1835. 2 pieces.

697 Greenhow, Robert. Author of "History of Oregon and
California." A. L. S. 4to. 3 pp. Richmond, Nov.
19, 1821.

698 Greenleaf, Simon. American jurist and legal writer. Two
A. L's. S., 4tos, Portland, Aug. 18, 1827, and Cambridge,
Oct. 23, 1852. 2 pieces.

699 Griswold, Rufus Wilmot. American critic and editor. A.
L. S. 4to. New York, Sept. 17, 1851.

700 Grimke, Frederick. Author and judge. A. L. S. 4to.
2 pp. Chillicothe, March 9, 1838.

701 Grimke, Thos. S. American jurist, author and philanthropist. Two A. L's., 4tos, Charleston, May 17, 1831, and
July 2, 1832. 2 pieces.

702 HALE, SARAH JOSEPHA. American authoress. A.
L. S. 4to. Philadelphia, Sept. 13, 1850.

703 Hammond, Chas. Author. Wrote in defense of General
St. Clair. A. L. S. 4to. Cincinnati, Oct. 9, 1828.

704 Haven, Nathaniel A. American journalist and author.
A. L. S. 4to. Portsmouth, Dec. 21, 1825.

705 Headley, Joel T. American author. Two A. L's. S., 4to
and 8vo. Various dates.

706 Henry, Caleb S. American author. A. L. S. 4to. 2
pp. Hartford, Jan. 21, 1835.

707 Hentz, Caroline Lee. American authoress. A. L. S. 4to.
2 pp. Tuscaloosa, June 1, 1843.

708 Herbert, Henry W. ("Frank Forrester"). Poet, novelist,
critic, etc. A. L. S. 8vo. May 7, 1845.

709 Herndon, E. B, Lincoln's law partner. Author of "Life
of Lincoln." A. L. S. 4to. Springfield, Jan. 10, 1868.

710 Holmes, Oliver Wendell. Distinguished American author,
wit and poet. A. L. S. 8vo. May 21, 1860.

711 Holtzendorff, Franz von. German historian. A. L. S.
Small 8vo. 3 pp. Berlin, May 29, 1869.

712 Hooker, Herman. Theological author. A. L. S. 4to.
December 2, 1840.

713 Hunt, Freeman. Editor of *The Merchant's Magazine*. A. L.
S. 4to. 2 pp. New York, June 16, 1851.

714 Hunt, Sallie W. Authoress. A. L. S. 8vo. New Orleans,
May 9. No year.

715 INGERSOLL, ROBERT J. Author and atheist. A. L. S.
4to. Washington, April 24, 1823.

716 Ingraham, Joseph H. Novelist. A. L. S. 4to. Philada.,
July 5, 1839.

717 Inman, John. Journalist. Two A. L's. S. 4tos. New
York, Jan. 1841, and March 7, 1848. 2 pieces

718 Irving, Washington. Distinguished American author.
A. L. S. 8vo. Feb. 29. No year.

719 JAMES, WM. D. Author of "Life of Marion." Col. in
the Revolution. Judge of South Carolina. A. L. S.
4to. 3 pp. Stateburgh, Feb. 14, 1816.

720 James, Wm. D. A. L. S. 4to. Stateburgh, July 26, 1820.

721 KENNEDY, JOHN P. American statesman and popular writer. A. L. S. 8vo. Baltimore, March 2, 1864.

722 Kent, James. American jurist. Author of "Kent's Commentaries." Friend of Alex. Hamilton, Chancellor of New York. A. L. S. 4to. 3 pp. New York, March 29, 1797.

723 Kent, James. A. L. S. 4to. 8 pp. Aug. 22, 1787.

724 Key, Francis Scott. Author of "The Star Spangled Banner." A. L. S. 8vo. Washington, March 21, 1836. With address.

725 Key, Francis Scott. A. L. S. 4to. Washington, Nov. 1, 1837. With address.

726 Klipstein, L. F. Editor and author of "The Polyglott." A. L. S. April 25, 1845.

727 LAWRENCE, W. B. Editor "Wheaton's International Law." Three A. L's. S., 4tos. Various dates. 3 pieces.

728 Lea, Henry C. Author. A. L. S. 8vo. Phila., Feb. 6, 1871.

729 Leonard, Daniel. Author and Royalist. A. L. S. 4to. Bermuda, Feb. 19, 1803.

730 Lieber, Francis. Historical and political writer. A. L. S. 4to. Phila., May 14, 1834.

731 Lieber, Francis. A. L. S. 8vo. No date.

732 Longfellow, Henry W. Eminent American poet. A. L. S. 4to. 2 pp. Cambridge, March 17, 1866.

733 Longfellow, Henry W. A. L. S. 8vo. 2 pp. Cambridge, March 31, 1873.

734 Lowell, John. Political writer. One of the founders of the Boston Athenæum. Two A. L's. S. Folio and 8vo. Various dates. 2 pieces.

735 McCALL, HUGH. Author of the "History of Georgia." A. L. S. 4to. 2 pp. Savannah, Dec. 8, 1812.

736 McCall, Hugh. A. L. S. 4to. 2 pp. Savannah, Feb. 15, 1817.

737 McClung, Alex. K. Author. A. L. S. 4to. April 22, 1841.

738 Marsh, Geo. P. American philologist. A. L. S. 8vo. 3 pp. Washington, Nov. 22, 1846.

739 Martin, J. L. Political writer. A. L. S. 8vo. Paris, July 25, 1825.

740 Mathews, Cornelius. American *litterateur* and journalist. A. L. S. 8vo. 2 pp. New York, March 30, 1843.

741 Mayer, Brantz. Distinguished American writer. A. L. S. 8vo. 3 pp. Baltimore, Jan. 20, 1858.

742 Metcalf, Theodore. Legal author. A. L. S. 8vo. 2 pp. Boston, Jan. 24, 1863.

743 NEAL, JOHN. Poet and *litterateur*. A. L. S. 4to. Portland, Sept. 22, 1849.

744 Niles, Hezekiah. American journalist, and founder of "Niles' Register." Three A. L's. S., 4tos. Various dates.
3 pieces.

745 O'SULLIVAN, J. L. Editor *Democratic Review*. A. L. S. 4to. New York, Aug. 19, 1843.

746 PARKE, J. J. Distinguished English legal author. A. L. S. Folio. 7 pp. Oct. 29, 1825.

747 Parkman, Francis. American historian. A. L. S. 8vo. No date.

748 Parsons, Theophilus. Eminent lawyer and legal writer. Three A. L's. S., 8vos. Various dates. 3 pieces.

749 Pitkin, Timothy. American historical writer. A. L. S. 4to. 2 pp. Washington, Jan. 4, 1818.

750 Plumer, Wm., Jr. Poet. A. L. S. 4to. 2 pp. Epping, March 3, 1826.

751 RAMSEY, J. G. M. Historian. A. L. S. 4to. 2 pp. Charleston, Jan. 10, 1853.

752 Read, Thos. Buchanan. Distinguished American poet and artist. Autograph poem, signed ; sixteen lines, entitled : "The Great Are Falling From Us."
On the death of Daniel Webster.

753 Reynolds, Bernard A. Author of "The Life of Calhoun." A. L. S. 4to. Mobile, Dec. 18, 1860.

754 Renwick, James. Author and professor of chemistry and physics. A. L. S. 4to. New York, Oct. 30, 1850.

755 Richards, Wm. C. Author. A. L. S. 8vo. 3 pp. Providence, Sept. 18, 1863.

756 Ripley, Geo. Able American editor. A. L. S. 8vo. 3 pp. Aug. 30, 1853.

757 Robinson, W. E. ("Richelieu" Robinson). Founder of the *New York Tribune*. A. L. S. 8vo. 3 pp. New York, Dec. 14, 1855.

758 SAMPSON, WM. Author. A. L. S. Folio. New York, Sept. 28, 1813.

759 Sargeant, John O. Editor of the *New York Courier and Enquirer*. A. L. S. 4to. Washington, May 7, 1852.

760 Sedgwick, Theodore. Author and jurist. A. L. S. Folio. Nov. 18, 1831.

761 Sewall, H. D. Author of a compilation of hymns. A. L. S. 4to. New York, Nov. 16, 1826.

762 Skinner, Jno. S. Editor of *Plough, Loom and Anvil.* A. L. S. 4to. Baltimore, May 8, 1829.

763 Smith, Wm. Historian of New York and Chief Justice of New York before the Revolution. A. L. S., 4to, no date, and A. D. S., folio, New York, April 26, 1768.
2 pieces.

764 Smith, Wm. A. D. S. Folio. 15 pp. March 3, 1773.
Report of a committee, containing the reasons of the Council for not putting a stop to the execution of criminals convicted of counterfeiting.

765 Smith, Wm. A. D. S. Folio. 3 pp.

766 Sparks, Jared. Distinguished American historian and biographer. A. L. S. Boston, Sept. 30, 1834.

767 Sparks, Jared. A. L. S., 8vo, Cambridge, Nov. 30, 1864, and L. S., 4to, Cambridge, April 24, 1851. 2 pieces.

768 Sprague, Wm. B. Author and divine. A. L. S. 4to. Albany, March 1, 1833.

769 Spofford, A. R. Author, and librarian of Congress. A. L. S. 4to, May 29, 1865, and L. S., 8vo, May 12, 1874.
2 pieces.

770 Sullivan, Wm. American author. Two A. L's. S., 4tos, Boston, Dec. 26, 1833, and Jan. 24, 1834, and two others.
4 pieces.

771 Sumner, Geo. Traveler and author. Two A. L's. S., small 8vos. No dates. 2 pieces.

772 TAYLOR, BAYARD. Distinguished American traveler, writer and poet. A. L. S. Small 8vo. 3 pp. Jan. 8, 1848.

773 Tennyson, Alfred. Poet Laureate of Great Britain. A. L. S. 8vo. Jan. 18, 1854.

774 Thomson, C. W. Poet. A. L. S., 4to, Philada., April 17, 1843, and an autograph poem of two pages. 2 pieces.

775 Thomson, C. W. A. L. S. 4to. April 13, 1846.

776 Thompson, Jno. R. American *litterateur.* A. L. S., 8vo, Richmond, Dec. 5, 1855, and L. S., 8vo, Richmond, Nov. 22, 1855. 2 pieces.

777 Thompson, Waddy. Author. A. L. S. 8vo. No date.

778 Tomlin, John. Novelist. Two A. L's. S. 4tos. Various dates. 2 pieces.

779 Tripp, Alonzo. Author and lecturer. A. L. S. 8vo. 3 pp. Boston, Jan. 16, 1863.

780 Tuckerman, Henry T. Critic and miscellaneous writer. A. L. S. 8vo. 3 pp. New York, Jan. 6, 1868.

781 Tupper, Martin Farquhar. Popular English poet. A. L. S., with initials. 8vo. 3 pp. Philada., April 13. No year, and autograph poem of fourteen lines. 4to. 2 pieces.

782 Tyler, Robert. Author, and Register of the Confederate Treasury, 1861. A. L. S. 8vo. No date.

783 UPHAM, CHAS. W. Unitarian divine and writer. Two A. L's. S., 4tos, Salem, Jan. 19, 1847, and July 2, 1855.
2 pieces.

784 Upson, Anson S. Author and lecturer. A. L. S. 8vo. Nov. 15, 1865.

785 VERPLANCK, GULIAN C. Distinguished American scholar and writer. Three A. L's. S., 4tos, Dec. 15, 1849; Oct. 27, 1834, and Jan. 30, 1833; and A. L. S., in the third person, 4to, no date. 4 pieces.

786 WALKER, SEARS C. Astronomer and writer. A. L. S. 4to. Philada., Jan. 2, 1842.

787 Walker, T. Author of the "History of Ohio." 8vo. Nov. 12, 1841.

788 Walsh, Robt. Author. A. L. S. 4to. 2 pp. Baltimore, March 17, 1817.

789 Wheaton, Henry. American jurist and author. A. L. S. 4to. New York, April 20, 1827.

790 Whitehead, W. A. Author. Two A. L's. S. 4to and 8vo. Various dates. 2 pieces.

791 Whitman, Walt. American poet: author of "Leaves of Grass." A. L. S. 4to. 4 pp. Brooklyn, July 20, 1857.

792 Whitman, Walt. A. L. S. ("Walt" only). 4to. 4 pp. Brooklyn, July 28, 1857.
    This and the preceding letter are exceedingly characteristic of the man—"Wild, pathetic, nonsensical."

793 Whittier, Jno. G. Distinguished poet and abolitionist. A. L. S. 8vo. 2 pp. Feb. 2, 1840.

794 Wilde, J. W. Poet. Three A. L's. S. 4tos. Various dates.
3 pieces.

795 Wilde, Rich'd H. Author and lawyer. Two A. L's. S. 4tos. Various dates. 2 pieces.

796 Wood, Silas. Author. A. L. S. 4to. Washington, April 25, 1824.

797 YEADON, RICHARD. Editor of the *Charleston Courier.* A. L. S. 4to. Charleston, Nov. 19, 1835.

798 Young, John Russel. Distinguished journalist. A. L. S. 8vo. New York, Feb. 8, 1881.

WAR OF 1812 AND MEXICAN WAR.

799   **A**RMISTEAD, W. K. Brigadier-General. L. S. 4to. Jan. 19, 1819.

800   **B**LISS, W. W. S. Officer in the Mexican War. Three L's. S., 4tos, Monterey, Nov. 4, Oct. 20 and Nov. 1, 1846.   3 pieces.

801   **C**LAIBORNE, FERDINAND L. General in the War of 1812. A. L. S. 4to. July 17, 1812.

802   Combs, Leslie. Captain of spies in Dudley's Regiment, War of 1812. A. L. S. 4to. Lexington, June 24, 1839.

803   **D**ODGE, HENRY. General in the War of 1812. A. L. S. 4to. March 9, 1844.

804   **H**AMER, THOS. L. General in the Mexican War. A. L. S. 4to. Oct. 16, 1837.

805   House, James. General in the War of 1812. A. L. S. 4to. Baltimore, Dec. 9, 1805.

806   **I**ZARD, GEO. Major-General in the War of 1812. A. L. S. 4to. Oct. 12, 1812.

807   **L**EWIS, MORGAN. Served in the Revolution, Major-General in the War of 1812 and Governor of New York. A. L. S. 4to. Staatsburg, July 30, 1819.

808   Lowndes, R. Aide to General Gaines. A. L. S. 4to. Washington, April 25, 1821.

809   **M**ORTON, J. Major-General. Governor of New York. A. L. S. 4to. New York, Oct. 23, 1830.

810   **P**INCKNEY. THOS. Major-General in the War of 1812. A. D. S. Folio. Charleston, Oct. 30, 1813.

811   **Q**UITMAN, JNO. A. General in the Mexican War and Governor of Mississippi. A. L. S. 4to. Monmouth, Sept. 27, 1834.

812   **R**EALL, REAZIN. Brigadier-General in the War of 1812. Part of A. L. S. 4to. No date.

813 SCOTT, WINFIELD. Lieutenant-General. Distinguished in the War of 1812 and in the Mexican War. A. L. S. 8vo. Washington, July 2, 1846.

814 Swift, Jos. G. Brigadier-General. A. L. S. 4to. New York, May 14, 1825.

815 Swift, Jos. G. Three A. L.'s. S., 4tos. Various dates.
3 pieces.

816 TALCOTT, G. Officer in the War of 1812. A. L. S. 4to. Washington, March 25, 1840.

817 Twiggs, D. E. Major-General in the Mexican War. A. L. S. 4to. Fort Scott, Aug. 4, 1817.

818 WINDER, WM. H. General in the War of 1812. Commanded at Bladensburg. A. L. S. 4to. 3 pp. Baltimore, Jan. 18, 1803.

819 Worth, Wm. J. Major-General in the Mexican War. A. L. S. 4to. No date.

820 Worth, Wm. J. A. L. S. Folio. West Point, Sept. 25, 1820.

821 Worth, Wm. J. A. L. S. 8vo. 2 pp. No date.

ARTISTS.

822 CAFFERTY, JAMES H. Artist. L. S. 8vo. New York, Feb. 4, 1850.

823 Catlin, Geo. American traveler and artist. Autograph on a season ticket to the exhibition of his Indian Gallery.

824 Chapman, Jno. G. American artist. Painted "The Baptism of Pocahontas" for the rotunda of the Capitol at Washington. A. L. S. 4to. Liverpool, June 15, 1837.

825 Chapman, Jno. G. A. L. S., 8vo., and A. L. S. in the third person. No dates. 2 pieces.

826 Church, Frederic E. Eminent American landscape painter. A. L. S. 4to. 2 pp. New York, Dec, 14, 1854.

827 Cropsey, Jasper F. American landscape painter. A. L. S. 4to. New York, April 15, 1854.

828 DURAND, ASHER B. Eminent American painter and engraver. Engraved Trumbull's "Declaration of Independence." A. L. S. 4to. New York, April 24, 1854.

829 FALCONER, J. M. Artist. A. L. S. 3 pp. April 15, 1854.

830 GAY, W. ALLEN. American landscape painter. A. L. S. 8vo. 3 pp. Hingham, Feb. 15, 1852.

831 HART, WM. Artist. A. L. S. 4to. 2 pp. New York, April 21, 1854.

832 Huntington, Daniel. Distinguished American painter. A. L. S. 4to. 2 pp. New York, April 9, 1850.

833 Huntington, Daniel. A. L. S. 8vo. New York, Nov. 19, 1850.

834 INGHAM, CHAS. C. Eminent American portrait painter. A. L. S. 8vo. 2 pp. New York, June 7, 1855.

835 Ingham, Chas. C. A. L. S. 8vo. Feb. 23, 1861.

836 Ingham, Chas. C. A. L. S. 4to. No date.

837 MOUNT, WM. S. American painter of humorous subjects. A. L. S. 4to. Stoney Brook, May 25, 1854.

838 NEAGLE, J. Eminent portrait painter. A. L. S. 8vo. No date.

839 Neagle, J. A. L. S. 8vo. May 28, 1849.

840 OSGOOD, S. S. Artist. A. L. S. 8vo. No date.

841 PARKER, G. Engraver of portraits. A. L. S. 4to. New York, Feb. 7, 1837.

842 Peale, Rembrandt. Eminent portrait painter. Painted the portrait of Washington. A. L. S. 8vo. No date.

843 ROTHERMEL, PETER F. Eminent American painter. Painted the "Battle of Gettysburg." A. L. S. 3 pp. 8vo.

844 SARTAIN, JNO. Eminent American engraver. A. L. S. 8vo. Sept. 12, 1861.

845 Smith, Russell. Landscape and scenic painter. A. L. S. 4to. April 10, 1854.

846 Sully, Thos. Eminent American portrait painter. Two A. L's. S. Small 4tos. Various dates.

ACTORS, COMPOSERS, ETC.

847 BISHOP, SIR HENRY. Eminent composer. A. L. S.
8vo. No date.

848 Bull, Ole Bornemann. Celebrated violinist. A. L. S. 4to.
New York, Oct. 16, 1844.

849 Burton, Wm. E. Celebrated comedian. D. S. Small 4to.
Phila., Nov. 18, 1841.

850 Butler, Frances Anne, (Fanny Kemble). Popular English
actress and writer. A. L. S. 4to. Phila. No date.

851 CHARLES, JNO. O. Actor, clergyman and author.
A. L. S. 4to. No date.

852 Cooper, Thos. A. English tragedian. A. L. S. 4to. No
date.

853 FORREST, EDWIN. Popular American actor. A. L. S.
8vo. Phila. No date.

854 MAYWOOD, ROBERT C. Tragedian. A. L. S. 4to.
2 pp. May 21, N. Y.

855 NOAH, MORDECAI M. Dramatist and journalist.
A. L. S. 4to. New York, Nov. 2, 1842.

856 RONCONI, G. Celebrated baritone. A. L. S. 8vo.
2 pp. New York, May 11, 1858.

857 TYLER, ROYALL. Dramatist and jurist. Author of
the first American play. A. L. S. Folio. Sept. 4,
1796.

858 Tyler, Royall. A. D. S. 4to. Oct. 15, 1811.

859 WOOD, WM. B. Celebrated actor. A. L. S. 4to.
Phila., Sept. 10, 1839.

860 Wood, Wm. B. A. L. S. 8vo. April 22, 1852.

DISTINGUISHED CLERGYMEN.

861   BRECKENRIDGE, JOHN.   Distinguished divine. A. L. S. 4to. Washington, Aug. 26, 1818.

862   Bridge, Christopher. Clergyman of Boston. A. D. S. Small 4to. Oct. 18, 1702.

863   Burgess, George. Bishop of Maine. A. L. S. 8vo. Gardiner, Oct. 1, 1855.

864   CHANCHE, JOHN. Bishop of Natchez. A. L. S. 4to. 3 pp. No date.

865   Channing, Wm. E. Distinguished Unitarian divine, and most eloquent writer. A. L. S. 4to. Boston, Nov. 2, 1838.

866   Clark, Thos. M. P. E. Bishop of Rhode Island. A. L. S. Providence, Aug. 11, 1859.

867   Clay, Jos. Eminent divine. Two A. L's. S. 4tos. Different dates.   2 pieces.

868   Croswell, Harry. American journalist and clergyman. Two A. L's. S. 4tos. Different dates.   2 pieces.

869   ELLIOTT, STEPHEN. Bishop of Georgia. A. L. S. 8vo. No date.

870   FISK, PLINY. American missionary. A. L. S. 4to. 4 pp. Smyrna, Feb. 26, 1820.

871   HICKS, ELIAS. Founder of the Hicksite Quakers. A. L. S. 4to. 2 pp. New York, Dec. 29, 1792.

872   Hodge, Chris. Eminent theologian. A. L. S. 8vo. April 29, 1836.

873   JOHNS, JOHN. P. E. Bishop of Virginia. A. L. S. 8vo. April 28, 1835.

874   KEMPER, JACKSON. P. E. Bishop. A. L. S. 8vo. July 9, 1851.

875   Krebs, Jno. M. Distinguished divine. A. L. S. 8vo. New York, May 12, 1836.

876   MORSE, JEDEDIAH. American geographer and divine. A. L. S. 4to. 3 pp. Charlestown, Feb. 15, 1799.

877   PATTEN, WM. Distinguished clergyman. A. L. S. 4to. 2 pp. Hartford, Oct. 17, 1836.

878 Peabody, Ephraim. Distinguished Unitarian clergyman. A. L. S. 4to. New Bedford, Sept. 15, 1843.

879 Potter, Alonzo. Bishop of Pennsylvania. A. L. S. 8vo. 2 pp. Bethlehem, Pa., June 11, 1862.

880 Potter, Horatio. Bishop of New York. A. L. S. 8vo. New York, Oct. 19, 1855.

881 RODGERS, JOHN. Distinguished New York clergyman. A. L. S. 4to. 2 pp. New York, June 25, 1785.

882 Ryan, Patrick J. Archbishop of Philadelphia. A. L. S. 8vo. Sept. 26, 1851.

883 UPFOLD, GEO. Bishop of Indiana. A. L. S. 8vo. Indianapolis, April 17, 1860.

884 WOODS, LEONARD. Distinguished divine. Two A. L's. S. 8vo and 4to. 1834 and 1838. 2 pieces.

ATTORNEYS-GENERAL OF THE UNITED STATES.

885 AKERMAN, A. T. A. L. S. 8vo. Cartersville, Dec. 28, 1872.

886 BATES, EDWARD. A. L's. S. 8vo. No dates.

887 Berrien, Jno. Macpherson. Seven A. L's. S. 4tos. Various dates. 7 pieces.

888 Black, Jeremiah S. Secretary of State. A. L. S. 4to. Pittsburg, Nov. 17, 1856.

889 Black, Jeremiah S. L. S., 4to, and A. N. S., 4to. Different dates 2 pieces.

890 Bradford, Wm., Jr. Under Washington. A. L. S. 4to. April, 1784.

891 Butler, Benj. F. A. L. S. 4to. 2 pp. New York, June 8, 1846.

892 Butler, Benj. F. Five A. L's. S. and one L. S. 4to. Various dates. 6 pieces.

893 Bristow, Benj. H. A. L. S. 4to. Washington, July 1, 1876.

894 Breckinridge, Jno. A. L. S., in third person. 8vo. Dec. 21, 1803.

895 CLIFFORD, NATHAN. Justice of the Supreme Court.
A. L. S. 4to. Portland, May 7, 1853.

896 Clifford, Nathan. A. L. S. 8vo. Portland, Aug. 20, 1864.

897 Cushing, Caleb. Three A. L's. L. 4to. Various dates.
3 pieces.

898 DEVENS, CHAS. L. S. 8vo. Washington, June 5, 1879.

899 GARLAND, A. H. Three A. L's. S. 4to. Various dates. 3 pieces.

900 Gilpin, Henry D. A. L. S. 8vo. Aug. 17, 1856.

901 Grundy, Felix. A. L. S. 4to. Nashville, Aug. 10, 1823.

902 Grundy, Felix. L. S. 4to. Nashville, May 18, 1839, and indorsed check. 2 pieces.

903 HOAR, EBENEZER R. Two A. L's. S. 8vo and 4to.
Different dates. 2 pieces.

904 JOHNSON, REVERDY. Two A. L's. L., 8vo, and one L. S., 8vo. Different dates. 2 pieces.

905 LEGARÉ, H. S. A. D. S., folio, and A. L. S., in the third person, 8vo. 2 pieces.

906 Lee, Chas. A. L. S. Folio. 3 pp. Alexandria, Nov. 21, 1812.

907 Lee, Chas. A. L. S. 4to. Alexandria, July 30, 1795.

908 Lee, Chas. Autograph docket for the session of Court, 1794. 27 pp. 4to.

909 Lincoln, Levi. A. L. S. 4to. Worcester, Sept. 21, 1805.

910 Lincoln, Levi. A. L. S., 4to, Worcester, Oct. 19, 1797, and franked address. 2 pieces.

911 MASON, JOHN Y. L. S. 4to. May 2, 1844.

912 NELSON, JOHN. A. L. S., 4to, Washington, Dec. 14, 1844, and A. L. S., 8vo, April 14, 1843. 2 pieces.

913 PINKNEY, WM. A. L. S. 4to. Baltimore, Oct. 15, 1815. To James Monroe.

914 Pinkney, Wm. Two A. L's. S. 4tos. Different dates.
2 pieces.

915 Parsons, Theophilus. A. L. S. Folio. 3 pp. Byfield, Feb. 15, 1774. With address.

916 RUSH, RICHARD. A. L. S., 4to, Philada., April 17,
1833, and L. S., 4to, no date. 2 pieces.

917 Randolph, Edmund. Under Washington. A. L. S., 4to,
Feb. 20, 1794, and A. N. S., in the third person, 4to.
2 pieces.

918 Rodney, Cæsar A. A. L. S. Folio. 18 pp. Buenos
Ayres, May 22, 1824. To John Quincy Adams.

919 Rodney, Cæsar A. A. L. S. Folio. 3 pp. Wilmington,
May 21, 1817.

920 SMITH, ROBERT. Two A. L's. S., 4to and folio. Different dates. 2 pieces.

921 Smith, Robt. Three L's. S., 4tos. Various dates. 3 pieces.

922 Stanbery, Henry. A. L. S. 8vo. Washington, Feb. 5,
1867.

923 TAFT, ALPHONSO. A. L. S. 8vo. Cincinnati, Feb.
20, 1882.

924 Taney, Roger B. Chief Justice of the United States.
A. L. S. 4to. Baltimore, Sept. 26, 1827.

925 WILLIAMS, GEO. H. Two A. L's. S. 4to and 8vo.
Different dates. 2 pieces.

926 Wirt, Wm. A. L. S. 4to. 10 pp. July 20, 1822.
To the President of the United States, on the Georgia claims.

927 Wirt, Wm. A. L. S. 4to. Washington, Feb. 9, 1828.

CABINET OFFICERS.

928 Bibb, Geo. M. Secretary of the Treasury. Two A. L's. S.,
4tos, and one L. S., 4to. Various dates. 3 pieces.

929 Cabot, Geo. First Secretary of the Navy and President of
the Hartford Convention. A. L. S. 4to. Boston, Jan.
23, 1811.

930 Crawford, Wm. H. Secretary of the Treasury. A. L. S.
4to. 4 pp. Woodlawn, Jan. 29, 1833.

931 Crawford, Wm. H. A. L. S., 4to, 3 pp., and L. S., 4to,
Different dates. 2 pieces.

932 Ewing, Thomas. Secretary of the Interior. Three A. L's. S.,
4tos, and two L's. S., 4tos. Various dates. 5 pieces.

933 Granger, Francis. Postmaster-General. A. L. S. Folio.
Canandaigua, Nov. 6, 1816.

934 Thompson, Jacob. Secretary of the Interior. A. L. S. Folio. Oxford, May 18, 1847. With franked address.

935 Rush, Richard. Ten autograph legal briefs. Folios.
10 pieces.

936 Chase, Salmon P. Secretary of the Treasury and Chief Justice. A. L. S. 8vo. Oct. 14, 1869.

937 Chase, Salmon P. A. L. S. 8vo. Narragansett, Aug. 31, 1860.

938 Forward, Walter. Secretary of the Treasury. A. L. S. 4to. 2 pp. Jan. 10, 1831.

939 Wilkins, Wm. Secretary of War. A. L. S. 4to. 2 pp. Pittsburg, July 28, 1834.

940 Wilkens, Wm. A. L. S., 4to, 4 pp., Pittsburg, Oct. 23, 1819, and A. L. S., 4to, Washington, March 15, 1844.
2 pieces.

941 Campbell, James. Postmaster-General. A. L. S., 8vo, and L. S., 4to. Different dates. 2 pieces.

942 Graham, Geo. Secretary of War. Two A. L's. S., 4tos, Washington Oct. 3, 1823, and August 25, 1821. 2 pieces.

943 Marcy, Wm. L. Secretary of State. A. L. S. 4to. 3 pp. Albany, Feb. 2, 1826.

944 Livingston, Edw'd. Secretary of State. A. L. S. 4to. 3 pp. Jan. 26, 1796.

945 Eustis, Wm. Secretary of War; Governor of Massachusetts. A. L. S., folio, Boston, March 27, 1790, and A. L. S., 4to, Boston, May 27, 1792. 2 pieces.

946 Calhoun, Jno. C. Secretary of State and Vice-President. A. L. S. 4to. 2 pp. Fort Hill, June 28, 1842.

947 Clayton, Jno. M. Secretary of State. A. L. S. 4to. Washington, April 26, 1849.

948 Corwin, Thos. Secretary of the Treasury; Governor of Ohio. Two A. L's. S., 4tos, and two L's. S., 4tos. Various dates. 4 pieces.

949 McCrary, Geo. W. Secretary of War. Three A. L's. S., 4tos and 8vos. Various dates. 3 pieces.

950 Folger, Chas. J. Secretary of the Treasury. Six A. L's. S., 4tos and 8vos. Various dates. 6 pieces.

951 Brewster, Benj. Harris. Attorney-General. Two A. L's. S., 8vos. Different dates. 2 pieces.

952 MacVeigh, Wayne. Attorney-General. Three A. L's. S., 4tos and 8vos. Various dates. 3 pieces.

953 Henshaw, David. Secretary of the Navy. A. L. S. 4to. Washington, Aug. 31, 1843.

954 Blair, Montgomery. Postmaster-General. A. L. S. 8vo. December 30, 1868.

955 Callamer, Jacob. Postmaster-General. A. L. S. 8vo. Oct. 11, 1849.

956 Kennedy, John P. Secretary of the Navy. A. L. S. 8vo. Washington, Oct. 29, 1856.

957 Frelinghuysen, Frederick T. Secretary of State. A. L. S. 8vo. Newark, Oct. 20, 1865.

958 Southard, Sam'l L. Secretary of the Navy; Governor of New Jersey. Seven A. L's. S., folios and 4tos. Various dates. 7 pieces.

959 Spencer, Jno. C. Secretary of the Treasury. Two A. L's. S., 4tos. Different dates. 2 pieces.

960 Ewing, Thos. Secretary of the Treasury. Three A. L's. S., 4tos. Various dates. 3 pieces.

961 Campbell, Geo. W. Secretary of the Treasury. Three A. L's. S., 4tos, and L. S., 4to. Various dates. 4 pieces.

962 Upshur, A. P. Secretary of State. A. L. S. 4to. 3 pp. Oct. 28, 1825.

963 Upshur, A. P. A. L. S. 4to. No date. With franked address.

964 Sherman, John. Secretary of the Treasury. A. L. S. 8vo. Washington, Jan. 4, 1866.

965 Meigs, Return J. Postmaster-General. A. L. S. 4to. Nashville, Oct. 21, 1814.

966 Branch, Jno. Secretary of the Navy. A. L. S., 4to, and two L's. S., 4tos. Various dates. 3 pieces.

967 Badger, Geo. E. Secretary of the Navy. A. L. S. 8vo. May 11, 1841.

968 Dix, Jno. A. Secretary of War. General in the Rebellion. A. L. S. 8vo. New York, March 30, 1852.

969 Hamilton, Alex. Secretary of the Treasury. A. D. S. In full. Small 4to. Feb. 4, 1794.

970 Hamilton, Alex. L. S. 4to. Washington, Dec. 26, 1794.

971 Hamilton, Alex. L. S. 4to. Washington, April 17, 1790.

972 Seward, Wm. H. Secretary of State. A. L. S. 4to. Washington, March 20, 1852.

973 Hall, Nathan K. Postmaster-General. Three A. L's. S. 4tos. Various dates. 3 pieces.

974 Granger, Gideon. Postmaster-General. A. L. S. Folio. Whitesboro, Dec. 24, 1814.

975 Barry, Wm. T. Postmaster-General. Two A. L's. S. 4tos. Different dates. 2 pieces.

976 Kendall, Amos. Postmaster-General. Two A. L's. S. 4tos. Different dates. 2 pieces.

977 Smith, Caleb B. Secretary of the Interior. A. L. S. 4to. Washington, Jan. 27, 1862.

978 Forsyth, John. Secretary of State. A. L. S. 4to. Washington, March 12, 1830.

979 Dexter, Samuel. Secretary of the Treasury. A. L. S. Folio. Phila., Nov. 22, 1794.

980 Dexter, Samuel. L. S. 4to. March 18, 1801.

981 Gallatin, Albert. Secretary of the Treasaury. A. L. S. 4to. Washington, Oct. 26, 1815.

982 Butler, Benj. F. Attorney-General. Twelve A. L's. S. 4tos. Various dates. 12 pieces.
    Interesting series of letters.

983 Wolcott, Oliver. Secretary of the Treasury, and Governor of Connecticut. A. L. S. 4to. 3 pp. Washington, Nov., 16, 1800.

984 Wolcott, Oliver. Eight L's. S. 4tos. Various dates. 8 pieces.

985 Noble, John W. Secretary of the Interior. A. L. S. 4to. St. Louis, Oct. 1. 1880.

986 Dickerson, Mahlon. Secretary of the Navy and Governor of New Jersey. A. D. S. Folio. 3 pp. May 30, 1803.

987 Hazard, Ebenezer. Postmaster-General under Washington. A. L. S. 4to. Signed, Noel & Hazard. New York, Oct. 23, 1773.

988 Ingham, S. B. Secretary of the Treasury. Two A. L's. S. 4tos. Different dates. 2 pieces.

989 Thompson, Richard W. Secretary of the Navy. A. L. S. 4to. Columbus, Nov. 11, 1842.

990 Porter, J. M. Secretary of War. A. L. S. and L. S. 4tos. Different dates. 2 pieces.

991 Dallas, A. J. Secretary of the Treasury. Two A. L's. S., folio and 4to, and two D's. S. Various dates. 4 pieces.

992 Welles, Gideon. Secretary of the Navy. L. S. 4to. Washington, Feb. 8, 1864.

993 Duane, Wm. J. Secretary of the Treasury. A. L. S. 4to. Jan. 11, 1834.

994 Osgood, Samuel. Postmaster-General. A. N. S., third person. 8vo. No date.

995 Duval, Gabriel. Secretary of the Treasury. Two L's. S. 4tos. Different dates. 2 pieces

996 Crowninshield, B. W. Secretary of the Navy. L. S. 4to.
Jan. 30, 1818.
997 Harland, James. Secretary of the Interior. A. L. S. 8vo.
Washington, Jan. 9, 1873.
998 Guthrie, Jas. Secretary of the Treasury. L. S. 4to.
Nov. 9, 1853.

UNITED STATES SENATORS.

999 Gore, Christopher. Governor of Massachusetts. A. L. S.
Folio. Boston, Feb. 6, 1788.
Refers to the ratification by Massachusetts of the Constitution.

1000 Otis, Harrison Gray. Three A. L's. S. 4tos. Various
dates. 3 pieces.
1001 Rantoul, Robert, Jr. A. L. S., 4to, and A. L's. S., of
Robert C. Winthrop, Tristram Dalton, James Lloyd and
Nathaniel Silsbee, and L. S. of Rufus Choate. Various
dates. 7 pieces.
1002 Mellen, Prentiss. Four A. L's. S. 4tos. Various dates.
4 pieces.
1003 Foster, Dwight. Three A. L's. S., 4tos, and two A. L's. S.,
of J. C. Bates. Various dates. 5 pieces.
1004 Choate, Rufus. A. L. S., 4to, and A. L. S., of Benjamin
Goodhue. Different dates. 2 pieces.
1005 Sumner, Chas. Eminent orator. Five A. L's. S. 8vos.
Various dates. 5 pieces.
1006 Senators from Rhode Island. Albert C. Green, (2); Thos.
Foster, Ray Greene, (2); James Burrill, Jr., Christopher
Ellery and Asher Robbins, (7). A. L's. S. Various
dates. 14 pieces.
1007 Senators from Ohio. W. A. Trimble, Stanley Griswold,
Thos. Morris and Jacob Burnet, (4). A. L's. S. 4tos.
Various dates. 7 pieces.
1008 Senators from Ohio. Benj. Tappan, A. G. Thurman, (2);
Benj. Ruggles, (2); Wm. Allen and Sam. Huntington.
A. L's. S. 4tos. Various dates. 7 pieces.
1009 Senators from New York. Preston King, (2); Ira Harris,
(3); N. P. Talmadge, Daniel S. Dickinson, (2) and Henry
Foster. A. L's. S. 4tos and 8vos. Various dates.
9 pieces.
1010 Senators from New York. John S. Hobart, (3) and Nathan
Sandford, (4). A. L's. S. 4tos and folios. Various
dates. 7 pieces.

1011 Senators from Connecticut. Samuel W. Dana, (4); Wm.
W. Boarden, J. W. Huntington, Truman Smith, (2);
Jas. Lanman and Uriah Tracy.   10 pieces.

1012 Senators from Connecticut. David Daggett. A. L's. S.
Folios. Various dates.   9 pieces.

1013 Senators from Connecticut. Nathan Smith. A. L's. S.
Folios. Various dates.   12 pieces.

1014 Senators. Jno. P. Hale, (2); Simeon Olcott, Jeremiah
Mason, John Tipton, R. S. Field, J. W. Bradbury, E.
Shepley, Garret D. Wall, Wm. Gaston, Wm. B. Giles,
H. S. Geyer, Robert G. Harper, (2). A. L's. S. 4tos.
Various dates.   14 pieces.

1015 Senators. A. C. Hanson, (2); B. W. Leigh, Jeremiah
Mason, (2); Jas. Lanman, (2); E. F. Chambers, Jas.
W. Bradbury, Wm. Cocke, Geo. Poindexter, (3); Andrew Kirkpatrick, J. R. Underwood (3); R. S. Field,
and J. Holmes, (2). A. L's. S. Folios and 4tos. Various dates.   18 pieces.

1016 Senators. Dan'l E. Huger, J. S. Johnston, Alex. Porter,
Jonathan Roberts, Sam'l Houston. A. L's. S. 4tos.
Various dates.   5 pieces.

1017 Senators. Dan'l Sturgeon, (2); Jonathan Roberts, Willie
P. Mangum. A. L's. S. 4tos. Various dates. 4 pieces.

1018 Senators. Jesse B. Thomas, Sidney Bruce, (3); Wm.
Gaston, Asa Biggs, (2); Jas. Semple, Rich'd M. Young,
(2); Geo. Jones, (2); W. B. Bullock, C. Tait, Thos. W.
Cobb, W. Salisbury, (2); Eugene B. Cassidy, J. H.
Mitchell, Chas. C. Scott, C. C. Clay, B. Thurston, J. R.
Underwood, Jesse Bledsoe, (2); Garrett Davis, John
Rowan (2) and Geo. G. Wright. A. L's. S. 8vos and
4tos. Various dates.   29 pieces.

1019 Senators. B. Swift, Horatio Seymour, Sam'l S. Phelps,
Jonathan Robinson, Stephen R. Bradley, Jas. Fisk,
Dudley Chase, Sam'l Prentiss, Thos. J. Rusk, (2); Wm.
L. Dayton, Jno. Rutherford, Garrett D. Wall, (3);
Rich'd S. Field, (2) and Thos. Frelinghuysen. A. L's. S.
Folios and 4tos. Various dates.   18 pieces.

1020 Stockton, Rich'd S., from New Jersey. Seventeen A. L's. S.,
folios and 4tos. Various dates.   17 pieces.

1021 Senators. J. McIlvaine, Thos. Frelinghuysen, Wm. C.
Preston, A. P. Butler, R. B. Rhett, Joseph J. Evans, (2);
H. S. Guyer, Pohatan Ellis, (2); S. Adams, (2), Jas. F.
Trotter, Alpheus Felch, E. F. Chambers, (5); J. Pearce,
Rob't G. Harper, (3); B. W. Leigh and W. C. Rives.
A. L's. S. 4tos and folios. Various dates. 25 pieces.

1022 Senators. Jno. W. Daniels, (3); Wm. M. Gwin, J. M. Howard, H. S. Guyer, Martin D. Hardin, Rob't Y. Hayne, Simeon Olcott, J. W. McIlvaine, Wm. Logan, G. Poindexter, (2); Jno. Henderson, Trusten Polk, H. W. Blair, J. A. Bayard, D. E. Noble, (2); Jno. Williams, (2); Jno. W. Thompson, Jno. R. Thompson, David L. Morris, A. C. Dodge, Jas. Cooper, Rob't G. Harper, (2). A. L's. S. 4tos and folios. Various dates. 29 pieces.

1023 Senators. H. M. Rice, A. S. Porter, (2); Sam'l C. Pomeroy, Cornelius Cole, David T. Patterson, J. Harris, D. L. Yulee, Jno. Codman, Jno. A. Collier, D. M. Forney, Rob't H. Goldsborough, (2); H. L. Hosmer, Thos. Lowndes, (2); R. W. Gibbs, W. Lowndes, James Lovell, Jas. Noble, (2); Rob't Philson, O. H. Smith, (3); Jabez Upham, Solomon Foote, (2); Jno. Henderson, W. C. Preston, Wm. Upham, Rich'd Yates and seven others. A. L's. S. 8vos, 4tos and folios. Various dates.

35 pieces.

JUDGES OF THE SUPREME COURT OF PENNSYLVANIA.

1024 A GNEW, DANIEL. 1873. Two A. L's. S., 8vos. Different dates. 2 pieces.

1025 Allen, Wm. 1767. A. D. S., small 4to., Jan. 19, 1756, and D. S., small 4to, Oct. 20, 1741. 2 pieces.

1026 Armstrong, James. 1857. Two A. L's. S., 4tos. Different dates. 2 pieces.

1027 Atlee, Wm. A. 1777. A. D. S., Folio, Feb. 23, 1792, and two D's. S., folios, different dates. 3 pieces.

1028 B LACK, JEREMIAH S. 1851. A. L. S. Folio. Lancaster, March 23, 1840.

1029 Brackenridge, Hugh H. 1799. A. L. S. 4to. Oct. 14, 1791.

1030 Brackenridge, Hugh H. A. L. S., 4to, Aug. 1, 1802, and A. L. S. (third person), 4to, no date. 2 pieces.

1031 Bradford, Wm. 1791. Two A. D's. S., 4to and folio. Different dates. 2 pieces.

1032 Bryan, Geo. 1780. President of the Supreme Executive Council of Pennsylvania and member of the Stamp Act Congress of 1765. A. L. S. Folio. Lancaster, May 16, 1789.

1033   Burnside, Thos. 1845. A. L. S. Folio. Bellefonte, Jan. 6, 1823.

1033a   CHAMBERS, GEO. 1851. A. L. S. 4to. July 28, 1821.

1033b   Chew, Benjamin. 1774. A. L. S., 4to, April 26, 1770 and D. S., 4to, April 2, 1754.   2 pieces.

1033c   Clark, Silas M. 1882. A. L. S. 8vo. 2 pp. No date.

1034   Coleman, Wm. 1758. Two D's. S., small 4tos. Different dates.   2 pieces.

1035   DEAN, JOHN. A. L. S. 4to. Nov. 29, 1893.

1036   Duncan, Thos. 1817. A. L. S. Folio. Carlisle, April 8, 1808.

1037   Duncan, Thos. 1817. A. L. S. 4to. Carlisle, Sept. 12, 1810.

1038   FELL, D. NEWTON. Two A. L's. S., 8vos. Different dates.   2 pieces.

1039   GIBSON, JOHN B. 1827. A. L. S. 4to. 3 pp. No date.

1040   Gibson, John B. A. L. S. 4to. Lancaster, Nov. 13, 1831.

1041   Green, Henry. 1881. Two A. L's. S., 8vos. Different dates.   2 pieces.

1042   Growden. Lawrence. 1750. A. D. S. Oblong 4to. No date.

1043   HUSTON, CHARLES. 1826. A. L. S. 4to. Dec. 12, 1800.

1044   KENNEDY, JOHN. 1830. Three A. L's. S., 4tos. Various dates.   3 pieces.

1045   LANGHORNE, JEREMIAH. 1739. Parchment D. S. 4to. Dec. 28, 1729.

1046   Langhorne, Jeremiah. D. S. 4to. No date.

1047   Lawrence, John. 1767. D. S. Folio. Sept. 1, 1784.

1048   Lewis, Ellis. 1854. A. L. S. 8vo. Philadelphia, March 20, 1857.

1049   Lloyd, David. 1717. A. D. 4to. March 1, 1726.

1050   Logan, James. 1731. President of the Council. A. L. S. 8vo. May 28, 1733.

1051   Logan, James. A. L. S. 4to. 2 pp. Stenton, Dec. 23, 1733–4.

1052   Logan, James. A. D. S. Small 4to. June 26, 1731.

1053   Lowrie, Walter H. 1857. A. L. S. 8vo. Pittsburg, Nov. 9, 1860, and D. S., 4to. No date.   2 pieces.

1054 McKEAN, THOMAS. 1777. Signer of the Declaration of Independence and Gov. of Penn. A. D. S., 4to., Newton, May 25, 1779, and D. S., 4to. (signed both by McKean and his wife), Phila., Jan. 2, 1794.

1055 McKean, Thomas. A. D. S. 4to. No date.

1055½ McCollum, Jos. B. A. L. S. 8vo. Philada., Jan. 30. No year.

1056 NORRIS, ISAAC. (Declined) 1731. D. S. Feb. 17, 1761.

1057 Norris, Isaac. Parchment. D. S. Folio. Nov. 30, 1717.

1058 PAXSON, EDWARD M. 1874. Two A. L's. S. 8vos. Different dates. 2 pieces.

1059 Porter, Wm. A. 1858. L. S. 4to, and two D's. S., 4tos. Various dates. 3 pieces.

1060 REED, JOHN M. 1858. Two A. L's. S. 4tos. Different dates. 2 pieces.

1061 Reed, Jos. (Declined) 1777. President of Penna. D. S. 4to. Phila., Sept. 18, 1779.
Governor Bryan's receipt for salary, as Vice-President of Penna.

1062 Rodgers, Molton C. 1826. A. L. S. 4to. Lancaster, Feb. 28, 1817.

1063 Rush, Jacob. 1784. A. L. S. 4to. 2 pp. Reading, Dec. 6, 1798. With address.

1064 Rush, Jacob. A. L. S. 4to. 2 pp. Reading, Oct. 10, 1798. With address.

1065 SERGEANT, THOMAS. 1834. A. L. S. Folio. Harrisburg, Dec. 10, 1818.

1066 Sharswood, Geo. 1878. Four A. L's. S. 8vos. Various dates. 4 pieces.

1067 Shippen, Edward. 1799. A. L. S. 4to. Phila., Jan. 20, 1787. With address.

1068 Shippen, Edward. Parchment. D. S. Folio. July 24, 1800. Signed also Thomas Smith, M. O. C.

1069 Smith, Frederick. 1828. A. L. S. Reading, Oct. 13, 1811.

1070 Smith, Thomas. 1794. Member of the Continental Congress. A. L. S. 4to. Bedford, July 19, 1773.

1071 Smith, Thomas. A. L. S. 4to. 2 pp. Carlisle, Oct. 20, 1788. With address.

1072 Sterrett, James P. 1877. Three A. L's. S. 8vos. Various dates. 3 pieces.

1073 Strong, Wm. 1857. A. L. S. 8vo. Phila., Sept. 21, 1869.

1074 THOMPSON, JAMES. 1867. Two A. L's. S. 8vos.
Different dates. 2 pieces.

1075 Tilghman, Wm. 1806. A. L. S. 4to. Phila., April 1, 1805.

1076 Tilghman, Wm. A. L. S. 4to. Phila., Aug. 9, 1820.

1077 Tilghman, Wm. A. L. S. 4to. Chestnut Hill, March 13, 1806.

1078 Tod, John. 1827. A. L. S. 4to. Bedford, Feb. 3, 1820.

1079 WILLIAMS, HENRY W. 1887. Two A. L's. S. 8vos. Different dates. 2 pieces.

1080 Willing, Thomas. 1767. D. S. 4to. Feb. 6, 1792.

1081 Woodward, Geo. W. 1863. A. L. S. 8vo. Phila., Easter, 1853.

1082 YEATES, JASPER. 1791. A. L. S. 4to. Lancaster, Sept. 21, 1781. Signed also by Geo. Ross.

1083 Ycates, Jasper. Two A. D's. S. 4tos. Different dates.
2 pieces.

MISCELLANEOUS.

1084 AMES, FISHER. Distinguished statesman and orator. A. L. S. 4to. Dedham, Dec. 17, 1795. With address.

"I have been full of impatience to hear the first doings of the house, I am consoled by your opinion that matters will not be the worst possible. All is at risk in the point of our three branches remaining true & firm in the defense of gov't. A cowardly or divided spirit now would set all afloat again. The strength of faction lies more in the power to intimidate than to overcome the constituted authorities. The clamor against the treaty is over even in Boston, which may be termed the bell tower where anarchy rings the tocsin. In the country, the acts of our Jacobins went no further than to raise some vapors to cloud the minds of the people, but no heat, they were puzzled, and are not yet perhaps enlightened, but are not enflamed. It is vain to expect those who get wrong by the sudden impulse of feeling will get right by the tiresome labor of reasoning. Yet all who do reason are convinced & those who do not begin to be cool even in Boston & to take their opinions on trust, that is getting right as they get wrong."

1085 Austin, James T. Wrote the life of "Elbridge Gerry." Attorney-General of Massachusetts. A. L. S. 4to. Boston, Sept. 19, 1844.

1086 BEAUMONT, WM. Celebrated surgeon. A. L. S. Folio. Fort Howard, Nov. 18, 1826.

1087 Beck, John B. Scientist. A. L. S. 4to. New York, Dec. 6, 1838.

1088 Beck, Lewis C. Scientist. A. L. S. 8vo. No date.

1089   Bibb, Wm. W.   Secretary of the Treasury and Governor of Alabama. D. S. Folio. Nov. 12, 1818.

1090   Bigler, John.   Governor of California. A. L. S. 4to. · May 13, 1852.

1091   Botts, John M., of Virginia. Distinguished statesman. A. L. S. 4to. Nov. 13, 1865.

1092   Brady, James T.   Distinguished New York lawyer. A. L. S. 8vo. New York, Jan. 19, 1859.

1093   Bourne, Benj.   Officer in the Revolution; crossed the Delaware with Washington; member of the first Congress, and Judge of Rhode Island. A. L. S. Folio. Philadelphia, Dec. 21, 1790.

1094   Bourne. Benj.   D. S. Folio. Feb. 9, 1782.

      Draft of a letter from the Governor of Rhode Island to General Lincoln, in reference to the defense of Newport. Copied by order of the Legislature of Rhode Island, February 9, 1782.

1095   Bourne, Benj.   Five A. L's. S., folios and 4tos. Various dates.   5 pieces.

1096   Burr, Aaron.   Vice-President of the United States. Killed Alex. Hamilton in a duel. A. L. S. 4to. 2 pp. New York, Dec. 12, 1790. With address.

1097   Burden, Henry.   Inventor of Burden's steamboat. A. L. S. Folio. Nov. 5, 1830.

1098   Burges, Tristam.   Orator, and Chief Justice of Rhode Island. Three A. L's. S., folios and 4tos. Various dates.   3 pieces.

1099   Burrows, Wm.   Colonial Chief Justice of South Carolina. Four D's. S., folios. Various dates.   4 pieces.

1100   CARPENTER, MATT. H.   President *pro tem.* of the United States Senate. A: L. S. 8vo. March 11, 1866.

1101   Chapman, Nathaniel.   Eminent physician. A. L. S. 4to. Philada., March 24, 1823.

1102   Cheves, Langdon.   American statesman; Speaker of the House. Two A. L's. S., 4to, Sept. 8 and Nov. 3, 1820.   2 pieces.

1103   Clinton, De Witt.   Governor of New York. A. D. S. Folio. No date.

1104   Conner, David.   Commodore in the United States Navy. A. L. S. 8vo. Philada., Oct. 23, 1850.

1105   DANDRIDGE, BARTHOLOMEW.   Washington's private secretary. A. L. S. 4to. 4 pp. New Kent, March 7, 1781. To Colonel Wadsworth.

      Interesting letter, mentioning General Washington and complaining of the French troops being quartered on Mr. Custis's estate.

1106 Detmold, C. E. Engineer and architect. Built Crystal Palace, N. Y., 1852. A. L. S. 4to. Feb., 1851.

1107 Dickinson, Philemon. Governor of New Jersey. A. L. S. 4to. Dec. 21, 1838.

1108 Dwight, Theodore. Secretary of the Hartford Convention. A. L. S. 4to. New York, April 17, 1834.

1109 Dix, Miss Dorothea. Philanthropist. A. N. S., in the third person. 8vo. Feb. 18, 1853.

1110 EMMET, THOMAS ADDIS. Eloquent Irish lawyer; leader of the "United Irishmen." Six A. L's. S., folios and 4tos. Various dates. 6 pieces.

1111 Ewing, James. Brigadier-General in the Revolution. D. S. 4to. Philada., Sept., 1784.

1112 FOSTER, ISAAC. Massachusetts patriot and physician. A. D. S. (signature in the body). 4to. 2 pp. 1774.

1113 GALUSHA, JONAS. Governor of Vermont. A. L. S. 4to. Windsor, Nov. 1, 1793.

1114 Giddings, Joshua R. Distinguished Abolitionist. Autograph sentiment, signed. 4to. Montreal, Dec. 26, 1862.

1115 Gould, B. A. Astronomer. A. L. S. 8vo. 2 pp. Boston, May 20, 1847.

1116 Guiteau, Chas. Assassin of Garfield. Signature and five lines written by request, while in the United States jail. Dec. 11, 1881.

1117 HOAR, SAM'L. M. C. from Massachusetts. A. L. S. 4to. Concord, Sept. 6, 1832.

1118 Hilliard, Geo. S. Orator and writer. A. L. S. 8vo. No date.

1119 Hoffman, John T. Governor of New York. A. L. S. 4to. New York, June 30, 1863.

1120 Holmes, John. M. C. from Maine. A. L. S. 4to. 3 pp. July 28, 1823.

1121 Hall, Hiland. Governor of Vermont. A. L. S. Folio. Burlington, May 22, 1833.

1122 Harris, Elisha. Governor of Rhode Island. L. S. 4to. Feb., 1848. To the Governor of Alabama.

> Conveying the resolutions of the General Assembly of Rhode Island, in reference to the war with Mexico.

1123 Hendricks, Wm. Governor of Indiana. L. S. 4to. Indianapolis, Feb. 5, 1825.

> Conveying the resolutions of the Legislature of Indiana against the anti-slavery amendment to the Constitution of the United States.

1124 Howard, Geo. Governor of Maryland. L. S. 4to. Annapolis, June, 1832.

> Covering the resolutions of the Legislature of the State of Maryland,
> adverse to the re-election of Andrew Jackson, President of the United
> States.

1125 Hume, Joseph. British statesman. A. L. S. 8vo. 2 pp.
London, July 3, 1840.

1126 Huntington, Samuel. Governor of Ohio. A. L. S. 4to.
3 pp. Sept. 4, 1810.

1127 JOHNSON, H. Governor of Louisiana. L. S. 4to.
New Orleans, Feb. 1, 1826.

> Covering the resolutions of the Legislature of Louisiana, against the
> anti-slavery amendment to the Constitution of the United States, pro-
> posed by Georgia.

1128 Jones, James. Made an effort in the Georgia Legislature,
in 1796, to abolish the slave trade. A. L. S. 4to. 2 pp.
Louisville, Feb. 8, 1796.

> The letter mentions an effort which was made in the Legislature to stop
> the importation of negroes.

1129 Jones, Sam'l. Father of the New York Bar; Recorder of
New York. A. L. S. 4to. New York, Nov. 24, 1767.

> Mentions persons fined for voting in Dutchess Co., in 1766.
> Samuel Jones is placed in some list of the members of the Old Congress.

1130 Jones, Sam'l. Two A. L.'s. S., 4to and folio. Different
dates. 2 pieces.

1131 KELLY, JOHN. New York "boss" and prize-fighter.
A. L. S. 4to. New York, Nov. 29, 1855.

> "If I had been there it might have been different." Communicated
> from the Spiritual World, November 7, 1894.

1132 Kennedy, Joseph C. G. Statistician. A. L. S. 4to.
Washington, Dec. 24, 1849.

1133 Kerr, Michael C. Speaker of the House of Representatives. Three A. L's. S., 8vos and 4tos. Various dates.
3 pieces.

1134 LEWIS, MORGAN. Governor of New York. Served
in the Revolution; Major-General in the War of 1812
and Chief Justice of New York. A. L. S. Folio.
New York, Jan. 22, 1828. With address.

1135 Lewis, Morgan. A. D. S. Folio. No date.

1136 Lockwood, Joshua. One of the first Provincial Congress
of South Carolina. D. S. 4to. No date.

1137 Lowell, John, of Boston. Minister. A. L. S. 4to. New-
bury, April 13, 1743. To Rev. Jos. Whipple.

> Requesting that he unite in wedlock, without delay, James Atkin and
> Mrs. Mary Titcomb, "being tenderly concerned for the family."

1138 Lowell, John, Jr. Distinguished traveler, and founder of
Lowell Institute. A. L. S. 4to. Boston, July, 1832.

1139 Lamar, Mirabeau B. President of the Republic of Texas.
A. L. S. 4to. Austin, Feb. 27, 1840.

As President. " But that is not the point; the gist of the matter is, I
want to borrow *Two Thousand dollars*. I owe this amount in New
Orleans, for which I am weekly dun'd and dam'd."

1140 MADISON, DOLLY P. Wife of James Madison.
A. L. S., in the third person. 4to. Montpellier,
Sept. 9, 1737. With address and fine impression
of the Madison seal in black wax.

1141 Mattocks, Jno. Governor and Judge of the Supreme
Court of Vermont. A. L. S. 4to. Washington, April 5,
1826.

1142 Menard, M. B. Signer of the Texas Declaration of Independence. A. L. S. 4to. Galveston, Jan. 3, 1856.

1143 Mercer, John. Governor of Maryland. Officer in the
Revolution. A. L. S. 4to. Fredricksburg, Aug. 6,
1809.

1144 Minot, Geo. R. Wrote the " History of Massachusetts
Bay." A. L. S. Boston, Feb. 24, 1789. To Thomas
Dwight. With address.

Speaks of his history.

1145 Minis, Philip. First white man born in Georgia. A. L. S.
4to. Jan. 20, 1780.

1146 Mott, Lucretia. Abolitionist. A. L. S. Small 4to. No
date.

1147 Moorehead, James. American commodore. A. L. S.
4to. Aug. 8, 1842.

1148 Monteagle of Brandon, (Thomas Spring Rise), Lord.
Chancellor of the Exchequer. A. L. S. 4to. 2 pp.
Nov. 26, 1835.

1149 Murat, Achille. Author. A. L. S. 4to. New York,
Nov. 4, 1830.

1150 McClung, William. Kentucky pioneer and Judge. A. L. S.
Folio. May 6, 1789.

1151 NELSON, HORATIO, LORD. British naval hero.
Cut signature.

1152 O'CONOR, CHAS. Celebrated New York lawyer
and candidate for President. Two A. L.'s. S., 4tos,
New York, Sept. 17, 1858, and Sept. 5, 1845.

2 pieces.

1153 Otis, Harrison Gray. Member of the Hartford Convention. A. L. S. 4to. Boston, Nov. 21, 1825.

1154 Otis, Harrison Gray. A. L. S. 4to. Boston, Nov. 15.
No year.

1155   PALMER, SAMUEL. An Assemblyman. A. D. S. Small 4to. Hampton, Feb. 24, 1741–2.

1156   Perkins, Jacob. Eminent inventor. A. L. S. 4to. No date.

1157   Petigru, Jas. L. Distinguished statesman and unionist of South Carolina. A. L. S. 4to. July 8, 1822.

1158   Petigru, Jas. L. A. L. S. 4to. Charleston, Feb, 17, 1849.

1160   Pennington, Wm. Speaker of the House of Representatives. A. L. S. 4to. 2 pp. Newark, March 20, 1842.

1161   Phelps, Oliver. Purchaser of the "Genesee Country," in New York, and of the "Western Reserve," in Ohio. Ninety A. L's. S. Folios and 4tos. Various dates.
90 pieces.

> This interesting series of letters contains much important information relative to the purchase of the "Genesee Country" and the "Western Reserve." They date from 1777 to 1809, and are addressed to prominent individuals interested in that scheme.

1162   Prescott, Wm. Judge. Father of Wm. H. Prescott, the historian, and member of the Hartford Convention. Two A. L's. S., 4tos, and two L's. S., 4tos.   4 pieces.

1163   Poussin, Guillaume Tell. Distinguished French statesman. A. L. S. 8vo. May 6, 1852.

1164   Pilton, Nehemiah. Distinguished physician. A. L. S. 4to. Jan. 10, 1803.

1165   ROBINSON, EDWARD. Philologist and traveler. A. L. S. 8vo. New York, Oct. 19,1855.   •

1166   Reid, John Rae. Governor of the Bank of England. A. L. S. 4to. 2 pp. March 9, 1841.

1167   Ronaldson, James. Founder of Ronaldson's Cemetery, Philadelphia. A. L. S. 4to. 3 pp. Philadelphia, Oct. 7, 1835.

1168   Rotch, Wm., Jr. Celebrated Quaker merchant of Massachusetts. A. L. S. and L. S., 4tos. Different dates.
2 pieces.

1169   SERGEANT, John. Eminent American jurist and statesman. A. L. S. 4to. Washington, March 3, 1840.

1170   Sherman, Roger. Distinguished lawyer of Connecticut. Five A. L's. S., 4tos and folios. Various dates.
5 pieces.

1171   Smith, Israel. Governor of Vermont. A. L. S. Folio. Rutland, Dec. 7, 1807.

1172 Storrs, Henry R. Member of Congress from New York, A. L. S., 4to ; Erastus Root, member of Congress from New York, A. L. S., 4to, and eighteen other A. L's. S. of members of Congress from New York. Various dates. 20 pieces.

1173 Sullivan, Wm. Member of the Hartford Convention. Seven A. L's. S., 4tos. Various dates. 7 pieces.

1174 Smith, Gerritt. Early Abolitionist and friend of John Brown. A. L. S. 4to. Nov. 16, 1847.

1175 Smith, Gerrit. Two A. L.'s. S., 8vos. Different dates. 2 pieces.

1176 Swartwout, Sam'l. Great New York defaulter. A. L. S. 4to. New York, Nov. 17, 1830.

1177 TROUP, GEO. M. Governor of Georgia. A. L. S. Folio. No date.

1178 Truxtun, Thos. Celebrated American Commodore. A. L. S. 4to. 2 pp. Perth Amboy, April 10, 1804.

1179 Tucker, St. George. Member of the Annapolis Convention. A. L. S. Folio. June 2, 1826.

1180 Tucker, St. George. Three A. L's. S., 4tos. Various dates. 3 pieces.

.1181 VAN NESS, C. P. Governor of Vermont. A. L. S. 4to. 4 pp. Burlington, March 29, 1823.

1182 Vallandigham, Clement L. Virulent Secessionist. Two A. L's. S., 8vos. Different dates. 2 pieces.

1183 Vaughan, John. Philosopher and friend of Priestley. Six A. L's. S., 4tos and 8vos. Various dates. 6 pieces.

1184 WALPOLE, ROBERT. Earl of Oxford. Cut signature and portrait.

1185 Wheaton, Henry. Eminent jurist, legal writer and diplomatist. A. L. S. 4to. 4 pp. Copenhagen, Nov. 20, 1827.

1186 Warham, Chas. Prisoner on board the schooner " Packhorse." D. S. Small 4to, April 8, 1763.

1187 Williams, Lewis. The Father of the United States House of Representatives. A. L. S. 4to. Washington, March 18, 1820.

1188 Williamson, J. H. Governor of New Jersey. A. L. S. 4to. Elizabethtown, Feb. 3, 1838.

1189 YELL, A. Governor of Arkansas. Killed at Buena Vista. A. L. S. 4to. May 31, 1846.

PRESIDENTS AND VICE-PRESIDENTS.

1190 **A** DAMS, JOHN QUINCY. President. A. L. S. 4to. Washington, Sept. 26, 1817. With franked address and franked envelope.

1191 **B** UCHANAN, JAMES. President. A. L. S. 4to. Washington, Jan. 31, 1835. With franked address.

1192 Burr, Aaron. Vice-President. A. L. S. 4to. Albany, October 29, 1788.

1193 Burr, Aaron. A. L. S. (Initials.) 4to. No date.

1194 **G** ARFIELD, JAMES A. President. L. S. 4to. Washington, March 31, 1867.

1195 **H** ARRISON, BENJ. President. A. L. S. 8vo. Indianapolis, April 15, 1869.

1196 Harrison, Benj. A. L. S. 8vo. Indianapolis, July 23, 1867.

1197 Harrison, William Henry. President. A. L. S. Folio. North Bend, Dec. 28, 1839. With address.

1198 **J** ACKSON, ANDREW. President. D. S. Large 4to. Ship's papers, in blank.

1199 Johnson, Rich'd M. Vice-President. A. L. S. 4to. June 2, 1832.

1200 **M** ONROE, JAMES. President. A. L. S., 4to, Washington, Sept. 22, 1820, and franked address of Jas. Madison. 2 pieces.

1201 Monroe, Jas. A. L. S. 4to. Washington, Dec. 10, 1816. With address.

1202 **T** OMPKINS, DAN'L D. Vice-President. A. L. S., 4to, March 28, 1814; A. L. S., 8vo, June 21, 1814, and L. S., 4to, Albany, March 8, 1809. 3 pieces.

1203 **V** AN BUREN, MARTIN. President. A. L. S., 4to, Lindenwald, March 13, 1862; D. S., 4to, May 30, 1818; John Tyler, A. N. S., no date and A. L. S., 8vo, Dec. 22, 1841. 4 pieces.

1204 **W** ILSON, HENRY. Vice-President. A. L. S. 8vo. New York, Oct. 23, 1856.

COLLEGE PRESIDENTS AND PRO-FESSORS.

1205   **B**ATES, JOSHUA. President of Middlebury College. A. L. S. 4to. 3 pp. May 26, 1825.

1206   Beasley, Frederick. Provost of the University of Pennsylvania. A. L. S. 4to. 4 pp. Albany, Jan. 13, 1804.

1207   Buchan, John. Professor of Medicine. A. L. S. 4to. Charleston, July 9, 1815.

1208   **C**HAMBERLAIN, JEREMIAH. President of Oakland College. A. L. S. 4to. 3 pp. Jan. 20, 1847.

1209   **D**AVIS, HENRY. President of Middlebury College. A. L. S. 4to. May 30, 1810.

1210   Dew, Thos. R. President of William and Mary College. A. L. S. 4to. 3 pp. Nov. 26, 1855.

1211   **E**LLIOT, CHAS. W. President of Harvard College. A. L. S. 8vo. Cambridge, Dec. 9, 1881.

1212   **H**ALE, BENJ. President of Geneva College. A. L. S. 4to. Aug. 1, 1840.

1213   Hasbrouck, A. Bruyn. President of Brunswick College. A. L. S. 4to. April 25, 1839.

1214   Henry, Robt. President of South Carolina College. A. L. S. 4to. March 4, 1826.

1215   Holley, Horace. President of Transylvania University. A. L. S. Folio. New Haven, Jan., 1805.

1216   Humphrey, Herman. President of Amherst College. A. L. S. 4to. June, 1831.

1217   **L**EVERETT, JNO. President of Harvard, and Judge. A. D. S. Folio. 2 pp. No date.

1218   Longstreet, Augustus B. President of South Carolina College. A. L. S. 4to. Augusta, May 4, 1835.

1219   **M**ANN, HORACE. President of Antioch College. A. L. S. 4to. West Newton, Nov. 30, 1847.

1220   Messer, Asa. President of Brown University. A. L. S. 4to. 2 pp. Providence, May 2, 1806.

1221   Miller, John C.   President of the College of Jackson, La·
       Two A. L's. S., 4tos.   Different dates.   2 pieces·

1222   Millington, Jno.   Professor of Natural Philosophy.   A. L. S.
       4to.   No date.

1223   OLMSTED, DENNISON.   Professor of Chemistry
       and Astronomy.   Two A. L's. S., 4tos.   Different
       dates.   2 pieces.

1224   QUINCY, JOSIAH.   President of Harvard College.
       A. L. S.   4to.   Quincy, Oct. 1, 1856.

1225   SKINNER, THOS. H.   President of Andover Theo-
       logical Seminary.   A. L. S.   4to.   New Haven,
       Sept. 3, 1832.

1226   Smith, Jno.   Professor of Dartmouth College.   A. L. S.
       4to.   2 pp.   Oct. 12, 1778.

1227   WADDELL, MOSES.   President of Franklin Col-
       lege, Ga.   Three A. L's. S., folio and 4tos.   Vari-
       ous dates.   3 pieces.

1228   Walker, James.   President of Harvard College.   A. L. S.
       4to.   Jan. 2, 1840.

1229   Wheeler, P.   President of the University of Vermont.
       A. L. S.   4to.   Burlington, May 22, 1849.

1230   Williams, Elisha.   President of Yale College; member of
       the Albany Convention, 1754.   A. L. S.   4to.   New
       Haven, Nov. 9, 1736.   To Rev. Dr. Stephen Williams.

1231   Woodward, B.   Professor of Dartmouth College.   Small
       4to.   April 12, 1792.

1232   Woods, A.   President of the University of Alabama.   A.
       L. S.   4to.   June 15, 1831.

1233   Woods, Leonard.   President of Bowdoin College.   A. L. S.
       8vo.   No date.

ENGLISH JUDGES, ETC.

1234 Adolphus, John. Barrister and *littérateur*. A. L. S. 8vo. Nov. 13, 1807.

1235 Aguesseau, Henri François d'. Eminent French jurist. Chancellor of France. L. S. Folio. Paris, Sept. 3, 1710.

1236 Allen, John C. Chief Justice, N. B. A. L. S. 8vo. Nov. 8, 1870.

1237 Arden, R. P. First Lord Alvanley. D. S. Folio. Feb. 12, 1786.

1238 Bliss, Jonathan. Chief Justice, N. B. A. L. S., 4to, Dec. 12, 1821, and H. Black, Judge of Canada, A. L. S., 8vo. July 9, 1853.

1239 Blackstone, Sir Wm. Author of " Blackstone's Commentaries." A. L. S. 4to. 2 pp. Oxford, Oct. 10, 1765. With franked address.
   Fine specimen. Rare.

1240 Bosanquet, Chas. Distinguished English lawyer. A. L. S. 4to. Feb. 20, 1809.

1241 Brougham, Henry, Lord. Lord Chancellor of England. A. L. S. (Initials). 8vo. No date.

1242 Byles, J. B. Judge of Common Pleas. A. L. S. 8vo. 4 pp. London, Jan. 6, 1854.

1243 Camden, Charles Pratt, first Earl of. Lord Chancellor of England. A. L. S. 4to. Oct. 4, 1773.

1244 Campbell, John, Baron. Lord Chancellor of England. A. L. S. 8vo. No date.

1245 Coventry, William, Earl. Lord Keeper of the Great Seal. A. L. S. Folio. Sept. 1, 1637.

1246 Cowper, William, Earl. Lord Keeper of the Great Seal. A. L. S. 4to. July 5, 1714.

1247 Denman, Thomas, first Lord Denman. Lord Chief Justice of England. A. L. 8vo., 4 pp., and part of A. L. S., 4to. No date. 2 pieces.

1248 Duff, Chas. Judge of N. B. A. L. S. 8vo. Jan. 8, 1879.

1249 Egerton, Thomas, Lord Ellesmere. Lord Chancellor of England. Part of D. S. 4to. Signed also by John Sackville, Lord Buckhurst and Robert Cecyll, Earl of Salisbury. 1598.

1250 Eldon, John Scott, Earl of. Lord Chancellor of England. A. L. S. 4to. 2 pp. No date.

1251   Ellenborough, Edward Law, Lord.   Chief Justice and
        Counsel for Warren Hastings.   A. L. S.   4to, third
        person. Feb. 15, 1818.

1252   Egerton, Thomas, Lord Ellesmere.   Lord Chancellor
        of England.   D. S.   Folio.   May 3, 1615.   Signed also
        by Fulke Greville, Lord Brooke; Chancellor of the
        Exchequer, Sir Edward Coke; Duke of Suffolk and
        Edward Somerset, Marquis of Worcester.

1253   Erskine, Thomas, Baron.   Lord Chancellor of England.
        A. L. S.   4to.   Feb., 1797.

1254   Finch, Thos.   Lork Keeper of the Great Seal of England.
        A. L. S.   Folio.   2 pp.   April 30, 1651.   With address
        and seal.

1255   Finch, Thos.   Lord Keeper of the Great Seal of England.
        D. S.   Folio.   Aug. 21, 1674.

1256   Gurney, Russell.   Recorder of London.   A. L. S.   8vo.
        No date.

1257   Harcourt, Simeon.   Lord Chancellor of England. A. D. S.
        4to.   Aug. 5, 1697.

1258   Hardwicke, Philip Yorke, first Earl of.   Lord Chancellor
        of England.   A. L. S.   4to.   4 pp.   Feb. 17, 1735.

1259   Hardwicke, Philip Yorke, first Earl of.   Lord Chancellor
        of England.   D. S.   Folio.   May 15, 1755, and D. S.,
        4to.   2 pieces.

1260   Hargrave, Francis.   Editor of " Coke on Littleton."
        A. L. S.   4to, third person.   March 6, 1781.

1261   Lyndhurst, John Singleton Copley, Lord.   Lord Chancellor
        of England.   A. L. S.   8vo.   No date.

1262   Wedderburn, Alexander, Baron Loughborough and Earl
        of Rosslyn.   Lord Chancellor of England.   A. L. S.   4to.
        Feb. 12, 1801.

1263   Murray, William, Earl of Mansfield.   Lord Chief Justice.
        A. L. S.   4to.   4 pp.   May 19, 1744.

1264   Dundas, Henry.   Lord Melville.   First Lord of the
        Admiralty.   L. S.   4to.   4 pp.   Melville Castle, Dec.
        6, 1801.

1264½   Dundas, Henry.   Lord Melville.   D. S.   Folio.   Legal
        opinion.   Signed also by James Montgomery and David
        Greme.

1265   Paris, Frederick John.   Counsel for Wm. Penn in the
        case against Lord Baltimore.   A. L. S.   4to.   Aug.
        1736.   Addressed to the Hon. Thos. Penn.

1266   Paris, Frederick John.   D. S.   4to.   April 22, 1742.

1267   Wensleydale, James Park, Baron.   Baron of the Exchequer.
        A. L. S.   8vo.   No date.

1268 Plunket, William Conyngham, first Lord Plunket. Lord Chancellor of Ireland. A. L. S. 4to. No date.

1269 Pratt, Sir Jno. Lord Chief Justice, K. B. D. S. 4to. 1720.

1270 Raymond, Robert, Lord. Lord Chief Justice, K. B. A. D. S. 4to. Feb. 14, 1719.

1271 Abinger, Lord. (Whose proper name was James Scarlett). Baron of the Exchequer. A. L. S., 8vo, 2 pp., March 20, 1825, and D. S., 4to. 2 pieces.

1272 Tindal, Sir N. C. Chief Justice of England. A. L. S. 8vo. June 21, 1845.

1273 Wilkens, Lewis Morris. Judge of S. C. of Nova Scotia, A. D. S., 10 pp., folio; A. L. S. of Chas. Waters, S. C. of New Brunswick, and A. L. S. of John Westlake. 3 pieces.

1274 Yorke, Charles, Lord Morden. Lord Chancellor of England. A. L. S. 4to. 2 pp. Sept. 6, 1763.

1275 Yorke, Charles, Lord Morden. Lord Chancellor of England. A. D. S. Folio. 2 pp. Sept. 29, 1763.

CIVIL WAR.

1276 BARLOW, FRANCIS C. Brig.-Gen'l. Wounded at Gettysburg. A. L. S. 4to. New York, May 10, 1877.

1277 Barlow, Francis C. A. L. S. 4to. New York, Jan. 9, 1868.

1278 Barlow, Francis C. A. L. S., 4to, New York, May 6, 1868, and A. L. S., 8vo, New York, Aug. 25, 1869. 2 pieces.

1279 Barnes, Joseph K. Surgeon-General. A. L. S. 8vo. Washington, Jan. 19, 1864.

1280 Barry, Wm. F. Brevet Maj.-Gen. A. L. S. 4to. Buffalo, New York, Feb. 12, 1867.

1281 Benjamin, Judah Philip. Secretary of State of the Southern Confederacy. A. L. S. 4to. New Orleans, April 7, 1853.

1282 Blair, Francis P. Major-General. Through his efforts Missouri and Kentucky were saved to the Union. L. S. 4to. St. Louis, June 9, 1861.

1283 Blenker, Louis. Brigadier-General. A. L. S. 8vo. Nov. 21, 1861.

1284   CHALMERS, JAMES R. Confederate General. A. L. S. 4to. Friar's Point, Miss., Jan. 11, 1871.

1285   Chipman, N. P. Brigadier-General. Tried Wirtz. A. L. S. 8vo. Washington, Oct. 11, 1874.

1286   Cluseret, Gustave Paul. Brigadier-General. L. S. 8vo. New York, April 27, 1866.

1287   Cobb, Howell. Major-General in the Confederate Army. Speaker of the House of Representatives of the United States. L. S. 4to. Washington, Sept. 10, 1850.

1288   Conner, James. Brigadier-General in the Confederate Army. A. L. S. 4to. 2 pp. Columbia, Feb. 9, 1877.

1289   Cox, Jacob D. Sec'y of the Interior, Maj.-Gen. and Governor of Ohio. A. L. S. 8vo. Cincinnati, Jan. 14, 1880.

1290   Cram, Thos. J. Major-General. A. L. S. 4to. Detroit, Sept. 5, 1867.

1291   Crittenden, Thos. T. Brigadier-General. A. L. S. 8vo. Warrensburg, Jan. 25, 1867.

1292   DAVIS, JEFFERSON. President of the Confederacy. L. S. 8vo. Washington, Jan. 3, 1860.

1293   Davis, Thos. A. Brigadier-General. A. L. S. 4to. 2 pp. St. Louis, Feb. 28, 1863.

1294   Davis, W. W. H. Brevet Brigadier-General. A. L. S. 8vo. 4 pp. Morris Island, March 9, 1864.

1295   Devens, Chas. Brig.-Gen. and Att'y-Gen. of the United States. A. L. S. 8vo. Dec. 21, 1878.

1296   Douglas, H. K. Major on "Stonewall" Jackson's staff. A. L. S. 8vo. Hagerstown, July 23, 1874.

1297   Douglas, Stephen A. Statesman. Candidate for the Presidency. A. N. S. 8vo. Jan. 31, 1860.

1298   EWING, Thos., Jr. Major-General. A. L. S. 4to. Jan. 1, 1867.

1299   FORCE, M. F. Maj.-Gen. of Volunteers and Judge of Superior Court of Cincinnati. Six A. L's. S., 8vos. Various dates.   6 pieces.

1300   Frailey, Jas. M. Rear Admiral. A. L. S. 8vo. Philadelphia, May 15, 1866.

1301   HARWOOD, ANDREW A. Commodore. L. S. 4to. Washington, Dec. 22, 1862.

1302   Hovey, Alvin P. Major-General. A. L. S. 4to. 2 pp. Mount Vernon, Feb. 15, 1857.

1303   Hovey, Alvin P. Three A. L's. S. 8vos. Various dates.   3 pieces.

1304 JOHNSON, BRADLEY T. Confederate General. A.
L. S. 8vo. Richmond, April 13, 1869.

1305 Johnson, Bradley T. A. L. S. 8vo. Richmond, June 6. 1870.

1306 KANE, GEO. P. Chief of Police of Baltimore in the
Riot of 1861. A. L. S. 8vo. Baltimore, Jan. 4, 1867.

1307 MASON, JAMES M. Confederate Commissioner.
A. L. S. 4to. Washington, Jan. 14, 1855.

1308 Morgan, Geo. W. Brigadier-General. A. L. S. 4to.
Washington, Dec. 17, 1867.

1309 Mosby, Jno. S. Desperate Confederate partisan. A. L. S.
4to. Washington, Dec. 11, 1875.

1310 OWEN, JOSHUA T. Brigadier-General. A. L. S.
4to. 2 pp. Philada., Sept. 18, 1858.

1311 PAINE, HALBERT E. Major-General. A. L. S.
8vo. Washington, Feb. 12, 1866.

1312 Palfrey, Francis W. Brigadier-General. A. L. S. 8vo.
Boston, Nov. 5, 1866.

1313 Patterson, Robt. General in the Mexican and Civil Wars.
A. L. S. 4to. 2 pp. Philada., Feb. 15, 1834.

1314 Peabody, Chas. A. Provisional Judge of Louisiana; appointed by Lincoln. Two A. L's. S. 4tos. Different
dates. 2 pieces.

1315 Phelps, Jno. W. Brigadier-General. A. L. S. 4to.
New York, April 28, 1852.

1316 Phelps, S. Ledyard. Commodore. A. L. S. 4to. 2 pp.
Washington, June 12, 1854.

1317 Pettus, Jno. J. Confederate Governor of Mississippi.
D. S. (Commission). Oct. 15, 1862.

1318 Potter, Robt. B. Brevet Major-General. A. L. S. 4to.
Meadville, Jan. 22, 1868.

1319 Potts, B. F. Major-General, and Governor of Montana
Territory. Two A. L's. S., 4tos. Different dates. 2 pieces.

1320 Pryor, Roger A. Confederate Major-General. A. L. S.
8vo. 3 pp. New York, Feb. 21, 1870.

1321 Pryor, Roger A. Four A. L's. S., 8vos. Various dates.
4 pieces.

1322 REVERE, J. W. Brigadier-General. A. L. S. 4to.
Moristown, Jan. 16, 1864.

1323 Rogers, Horatio. Brigadier-General. A. L. S. 8vo.
Providence, Feb. 27, 1864.

1324   SANDS, JOSHUA R. Rear Admiral. A. L. S. 4to. 2 pp. Brooklyn, Nov. 5, 1849.

1325   Sanders, Geo. N. Blockade runner and Confederate Commissioner. A. N. S. 4to. No date.

1326   Schenck, Robt. C. Major-General and "boss" poker-player. A. L. S. 4to. 2 pp. Washington, Dec. 2, 1855.

1327   Schenck, Robt. C. A. L. S. Folio. Dayton, March 7, 1834.

1328   Stoughton, Wm. L. Major-General of Volunteers. A. L. S. 8vo. April 26, 1875.

1329   WALTHALL, E. C. Confederate Major-General. Six A. L's. S., 4tos and 8vos. Various dates.
                                          6 pieces.

1330   Wildes, Thos. F. Brigadier-General. A. L. S. 8vo. Athens, April 2, 1866, and two cut signatures of Brigadier-General Alpheus S. Williams.   3 pieces.

DISTINGUISHED AMERICAN JUDGES.

1331   Davenport, Abraham. Colonial Judge of Connecticut. A. L. S. 4to. Stamford, Feb. 25, 1744.

1332   Jones, Thomas. Judge of the Supreme Court of New York. A. L. S. 4to. 2 pp. New York, July 31, 1775.

1333   Jones, David. Chief Justice of New York. A. L. S. Folio. Sept. 14, 1773.

1334   Van Cortlandt, Stephanus. First native American Mayor of New York, 1677; filled almost every office in New York, with the exception of Governor. A. D. S. Folio. 2 pp. May 1, 1695.

1335   Washington, Bushrod. Associate Justice of the Supreme Court of the United States. A. D. S. Small 4to. July 1, 1805.

1336   Livingston, Brockholst. Officer in the Revolution and Associate Justice of the S. C. of the United States. A. D. S. 4to. March 28, 1783.
      Early signature "Henry B. Livingston."

1337   Black, Jeremiah S. Attorney-General and Secretary of State. A. D. S., with initials. 8vo.

1338   Nelson, Samuel. Associate Justice of S. C. of the U. S. A. L. S. 8vo. 2 pp. Cooperstown, Sept. 28, 1864.

1339 Bradley, Jos. P. Associate Justice of S. C. of the U. S. A. L. S. 8vo. Washington, Jan. 2, 1871.

1340 Field, Stephen J. Associate Justice of S. C. of the U. S. A. L. S. 8vo. 2 pp. New York, May 1, 1868.

1341 Fuller, Melville W. Chief Justice of the United States. A. L. S. 4to. Chicago, May 29, 1872.

1342 Morris, Lewis, Jr. Chief Justice of New York. A. L. S. 4to. Morrisania, July 8, 1729.

1343 Norris, Richard. Celebrated Judge, of New York. A. L's. S., 4tos, Albany, May 1, 1782, and March 22, 1802. 2 pieces.

1344 De Lancey, John. One of the first Provincial Council of New York, 1775–76. A. L. S. 4to. New York, March 14, 1798.

1345 Barnes, David L. U. S. District Judge of Rhode Island. Two A. L's. S., 4tos, 1792 and 1800. 2 pieces.

1346 Wendell, Oliver. One of the early Selectmen of Boston. D. S. Folio. June 3, 1795. Signed also by Sam'l Cooper. With fine seal of the city of Boston.

1347 Dawes, Thos. Judge of the S. C. of Massachusetts, 1792–1802. Four A. L's. S., 4tos. Various dates. 4 pieces.

1348 Parker, Isaac. Chief Justice of Massachusetts. Seven A. L's. S., 4tos. Various dates. 7 pieces.

1349 Sprague, Peleg. (The elder). Distinguished Judge of Massachusetts. A. L. S., 4to, Jan. 18, 1796, and Peleg Sprague (the younger), Judge, A. L. S., 8vo, Dec. 5, 1834. 2 pieces.

1350 Davis, Jno. Judge of the U. S. District Court of Massachusetts. A. L. S., 4to, Plymouth, April 27, 1779, and two other A. L's S. of the same person. 3 pieces.

1351 Wilde, Sam'l S. Judge of the S. C. of Massachusetts. Two A. L's. S., 4tos, 1807 and 1814. 2 pieces.

1352 Washburn, Emory. Governor and Judge of Massachusetts. A. L. S., 8vo, 2 pp., and A. D., 4to, 20 pp. 2 pieces.

1353 Allen, Chas. Massachusetts Judge and legal author. Six A. L's S., 8vos. Various dates. 6 pieces.

1354 Ward, Artemas. Chief Justice of Massachusetts. A. L. S., 4to; Marcus Morton, Chief Justice of Massachusetts, A. L. S., 8vo; Theron Metcalfe, Massachusetts Judge, A. L. S., 8vo, and Lincoln S. Brigham, Massachusetts Judge, A. L. S., 4to. Various dates. 4 pieces.

1355 Massachusetts Judges. Richard Fletcher, (2); Theron Metcalfe, Chas. Jackson (2), and Lemuel Shaw. A. L's. S., 4tos. Various dates. 6 pieces.

1356 Massachusetts Judges. Daniel Dewey, Dwight Foster, Benj. F. Thomas and Chas. Jackson. A. L's. S., folios, 4tos and 8vos. Various dates. 8 pieces.

1357 Massachusetts Judges. Lemuel Shaw (2); Pliny Merrick, Sam'l Putnam and Rich'd Fletcher. A. L's. S., 4tos and 8vos. Various dates. 5 pieces.

1358 Hosmer, Stephen T. Connecticut Judge. Four A. L's. S., various dates; six autograph charges to the Grand Jury, three autograph briefs and autograph sentence.
14 pieces.

1359 Connecticut Judges. Fifty-two A. L's. S., folios and 4tos; including Jonathan Ingersoll, James Gould, Thos. Seymour, Elizur Goodrich and Tappan Reeve. 52 pieces.

1360 Connecticut Lawyers who obtained prominence, and others. Twenty A. L's. S. Various dates. 20 pieces.

1361 Connecticut Members of Congress. Twenty-four A. L's. S., 4tos and folios; including Simeon Baldwin, Zetheniah Swift and Jonathan Brace. 24 pieces.

1362 Duer, John. Eminent New York lawyer and judge. Four A. L's. S., 4tos. Various dates. 4 pieces.

1363 Cowen, Ezekiel. S. C. Judge of New York. Four A. L's. S., folios, and D. S., folio. Various dates. 5 pieces.

1364 Emott, James. Eminent New York Judge. Eighteen A. L's. S., folios and 4tos. Various dates. 18 pieces.

1365 Woodworth, John. Judge of the S. C. of New York and author. Sixteen A. L's. S., folios, and three A. D's. S., 4tos. Various dates. 19 pieces.

1366 Conkling, A. Judge of the U. S. District Court of New York. Fourteeen A. L's. s., 4tos and 8vos. 14 pieces.

1367 Cady, Daniel. Judge of the S. C. of New York. Twenty-seven A. L's. S., folios and 4tos. Various dates. 27 pieces.

1368 New York Judges. Thirty A. L's. S., folios, 4tos and 8vos, various dates; including James Kent, Noah Davis, Chas. P. Daly, Aaron Hobart and John Duer. 3 pieces.

1369 New York Judges. Forty-two A. L's. S., folios and 4tos, various dates; including E. Cowen, Sam'l A. Foote and Ogden Edwards. 42 pieces.

1370 New York Attorneys-General and Chancellors. Twenty A. L's. S., 4tos and folios, various dates; including Wm. Kent, Jno. Willard, L. Tremain, Theo. Sedgewick, R. H. Walwroth, W. Kemp, T. J. Kemp. 20 pieces.

EMINENT PHILADELPHIANS.

1371 Francis, Tench. Revolutionary patriot. A. L. S. 4to. Sept. 23, 1786.

1372 Andrews, John. Provost of Pennsylvania. A. L. S. 4to. Sept. 2, 1794, and L. S., 8vo. No date.   2 pieces.

1373 Barton, Benj. S. Distinguished physician and author. A. L. S. 4to. June 1, 1812.

1374 Bingham, Wm. Member of the Old Congress. A. L. S. 4to. Phila., Nov. 29, 1796.

1375 Bingham, Wm. A. L. S. 4to. Phila., Feb. 17, 1799.

1376 Smith, Jonathan B. Member of the Old Congress. D. S. Folio. July 12, 1805. Signed also by Wm. P. Dewes, distinguished physician.

1377 Fisher, Miers. A. D. S. 4to. March 22, 1790. Indorsing the application of Anthony C. Duplaine, for Potash Inspector. Signed also by Duplaine.

1378 Girard, Stephen. Distinguished philanthropist. A. L. S. 4to. Phila., July 1, 1794.

1379 Graff, Frederick. Engineer. Erected the waterworks in Phila. Two A. L's. S. 4tos. Different dates. 2 pieces.

1380 Wharton, Henry. President of Common Council of Phila. A. L. S. 4to. Phila., Dec. 26, 1797. Signed by Francis Gurney, President of Select Council.

1381 Haga, Godfrey. Member of Select Council. D. S. Folio. Feb. 7, 1799.

   Report of a joint committee on the sum for which Councils should agree to part with the ferry on the Schuylkill. Signed also by the other members of the committee.

1382 Hallowell, John. Member of Select Council. D. S. Folio. May 2, 1799.

   Report of the committee relative to the sale of a site for a ferry over the Schuylkill. Signed also by Geo. Fox, John Connelly and Thos. Parker.

1383 Peters, Richard. Member of the Old Congress. D. S. Folio. Phila., March 28, 1800.

   Certificate of the Market Street Bridge Co., respecting two thousand shares subscribed by the mayor, aldermen and citizens of Philadelphia for the erection of a bridge.

1384 Latrobe, Benj. H. Architect. Designed the Bank of the U. S., etc. Three A. L's. S. 4tos. Various dates.
3 pieces.

1385 Lewis, Mordecai. A. L. S. 4to. Phila., Oct. 5, 1797.

1386   Nixon, John. Revolutionary patriot. Read the Declaration of Independence, July 8, 1776, to the people. A. L. S. 4to. June 9, 1800.

1388   Baker, Hilary. Mayor. A. L. S. (with initials). Folio. Phila., Aug. 17, 1797.   3 pieces.

       A letter in reference to, and the letters from Councils prior to purchasing the Health Office lot and buildings on the west side of the Schuylkill.

1389   Rafinesque, C. S. Scientist. A. L. S. 4to. Phila., Dec. 5, 1832.

1390   Ralston, Robert. Philanthropist. A. L. S. 4to. Phila., Nov. 3, 1813.

1391   Read, Jacob. City Solicitor. Two A. L's. S. 4tos. Different dates.   2 pieces.

1392   Roach, Isaac. Mayor. Served in the War of 1812. Three D's. S. 4tos. Various dates.   3 pieces.

1393   Ronaldson, James. Founder of Ronaldson's Cemetery. A. L. S. 8vo. Nov. 19, 1835.

1394   Sergeant, Jonathan D. Member of the Old Congress. A. L. S. Folio. Princeton, Dec. 26, 1775.

1395   Simpson, Henry. Author of "Lives of Eminent Philadelphians." A. L. S. 4to. Phila., Nov. 8, 1859.

1396   Vaux, Roberts. Mayor. A. L. S. 4to. March 4, 1819.

1397   Willing, Thomas. Mayor. Partner of Robert Morris. A. L. S. 4to. Phila., April 12, 1775.

1398   Wilson, Bird. Distinguished lawer and clergyman. Wrote the "Life of Bishop White." A. D. S. Folio. 2 pp. Feb. 7, 1803.

1399   Say, Benjamin. "Fighting Quaker." Founder of the College of Physicians. A. D. S. Small 4to. Philadelphia, 1779.   -

1400   Penrose, Chas. R. Celebrated lawyer. A. L. S., 4to., Carlisle, Dec. 15, 1832, and A. L's. S. of P. Physick, B. W. Richards, Blair McClenaihar, Peter Hagner, C. Cresson, etc. Folios and 4tos.   8 pieces.

1401   Irvine, James. Brigadier-General in the Revolution. D. S. 4to. Phila., Jan. 18, 1785.

1402   Mifflin, Thos. General in the Revolution and Governor of Pennsylvania. D. S., 4to, June 17, 1789; signed also by Geo. Ross, and D. S. by Christian Lower, Philada., April 1, 1784.   2 pieces.

1403 Nicholson, John. Comptroller of the United States Treasury. Two D's. S., 4tos, Philada., Sept. 30, 1791 ; signed also by Wm. Bingham and Jno. Donnaldson. 2 pieces.

1404 Francis, Tench. Revolutionary patriot. D. S., small 4to, April 7, 1797, and three others.   4 pieces.

1405 Willcox, Joseph. Member of the first City Councils of Philadelphia. Philada., June 6, 1692. To John Delavall. With address.

1406 Bayard, John. Member of the Old Congress and officer in the Revolution. D. S., 4to, Philada., Sept. 23, 1786, and two D's. S., 4tos, by Chas. Biddle, Geo. Ross and John Nicholson. Various dates.   3 pieces.

1407 Petition of property owners on Market (High) street to Select and Common Councils of Philadelphia, against the further erection of market-houses on High (Market) street. Philada., April 9, 1810. Signed by twenty-seven prominent merchants of the time.

1408 Kneass, Sam'l H. Engineer. A. L. S. Folio. Feb. 16, 1837. With a plan of the proposed draw-bridge in the vicinity of Gray's Ferry.

1409 Eminent Philadelphians. Robt. H. Rose, Joseph Shaw, Joseph R. Chandler, Hilary Baker (Mayor), Alex. Henry (Mayor), Henry Hillegas, Wm. D. Lewis, James Parker, Jno. Goddard, John Binns, Thos. B. Florence, Chas. B. Trego, Jno. Miller, Jno. Canan, Jno. W. Forney and others. Twenty-five A. L's. S., 4tos and 8vos, and eleven D's. S. and L's. S., 4tos. Various dates.   36 pieces.

1410 Eminent Philadelphians. Jos. R. Chandler, Jno. W. Forney, Henry Vethake, Chas. Biddle, Alex. Henry, Frederick Graff, W. D. Lewis, Benj. Matthias, Joseph Moland, Richard Alsop, Wm. B. Smith (Mayor), Dr. D. Hayes Agnew, Jno. Welsh, Wm. H. Allen, Paul B. Goddard, Jno. F. Watson, John Binns, and Chas. Gilpin (Mayor). Twenty-seven A. L's. S., 4tos and 8vos. Various dates.
                                                        27 pieces.

ATTORNEYS-GENERAL OF PENNSYL-
VANIA.

1411 Ross, Jno. 1738. A. D. S. Small 4to. April 6, 1761.

1412 Ross, Jno. Three D's. S., folios. Various dates. 3 pieces.

1413 Francis, Tench. · Two D's. S., folios. 1744 and 1749.
2 pieces.

1414 Chew, Benjamin. A. D. S. 2 pp. Feb. 19, 1787.

1415 Sergeant, Jonathan D. Member of the Old Congress.
Three A. D's. S., folio and 4tos. ¡Various dates. 3 pieces.

1416 Bradford, Wm., Jr. A. D. S.. Folio, 2 pp. 1790.

1417 Ingersoll, Jared. A. L. S., folio, Philada., Nov. 21, 1797,
and D. S., folio, no date. 2 pieces.

1418 McKean, Joseph B. Two A. D's. S., 4tos. Different dates.
2 pieces.

1419 Dickerson, Mahlon. A. D. S. Folio. April 23, 1804.

1420 Franklin, Walter. A. L. S. 8vo. May 28, 1796.

1421 Reed, Jos. D. S. 4to. April 23, 1818.

1422 Reed, Jos. A. L. S. 4to. April 28, 1811.

1423 Reed, Jos. A. L. S. 4to. Philada., April 7, 1817.

1424 Rush, Rich'd. A. L. S., 4to, May 2, 1808 and L. S., 4to,
Sept. 25, 1827. 2 pieces.

1425 Sergeant, Thos. A. L. S. 4to. Philada., June 24, 1826.

1426 Elder, Thos. A. L. S. 4to. Feb. 2, 1825.

1427 Smith, Frederick. A. D. S. 4to. Aug. 2, 1803.

1428 Douglass, Sam'l. A. L. S. 4to. Pittsburg, Aug. 15, 1818.

1429 Lewis, Ellis. A. L. S. 8vo. Philada., March 20, 1857.

1430 Todd, James. A. L. S. 4to. 3 pp. Uniontown, April
16, 1830.

1431 Reed, Wm. B. Three A. L's. S., 4tos, and A. D. S., folio.
Various dates. 4 pieces.

1432 Johnson, Ovid F. A. L. S., 4to; J. K. Kane, A. L. S.,
folio and two D's. S., folios; John M. Read, two A. L's. S.,
8vo and 4to, and four D's. S., folios and 4tos; Benj.
Champneys, two A. D's. S., 8vo and 4to; James Cooper
L. S., 4to; Thos. E. Franklin, two A. L's. S., 8vo and
4to, and D. S., folio. 17 pieces.

1433 Hughes, Francis W. Two A. L's. S., 8vos and L. S., 4to;
Wm. M. Meredith, six A. L's. S., 8vos and 4tos, and
two L's. S., 4tos; Benj. H. Brewster, six A. L's. S., 8vos
and 4tos; F. Carroll Brewster, three A. L's. S., 8vos;
Geo. Lear, two A. L's. S., 8vos; W. U. Hensel, A. L. S.,
8vo and L. S., 4to, and three others. 27 pieces.

PHILADELPHIA JUDGES.

1434 Ingersoll, Jared. Stamp Agent before the Revolution; Admiralty Judge, 1770. A. L. S. 4to. 2 pp. New Haven, Dec. 18, 1761. (Damaged).

1435 Lawrence, Thomas. J. C. P., 1745. Two D's. S. Small 4tós. 1751 and 1752. 2 pieces.
Signed also by William Plumsted, Mayor of Philadelphia, 1751.

1436 Hopkinson, Joseph. Judge, and author of " Hail Columbia." A. L. S. Folio. 2 pp. May 24, 1799. To Wm. Rawle. With address.

1437 Hopkinson, Joseph. A. L. S. 4to. 2 pp. Feb. 13, 1798.

1438 Hopkinson, Joseph. Three A. D's. S., 4tos. Various dates. 3 pieces.

1439 Hopkinson, Francis. Signer of the Declaration of Independence, Judge of the Admiralty. Wrote the " Battle of the Kegs." A. L. S. 4to. Navy Board, 25th Feb., 1777.
An order through Captain Bruster for cannon captured by Commodore Hopkins. Signed also by John Nixon (who read the Declaration of Independence to the people from the State House in Philadelphia), and John Wharton.

1440 Hopkinson, Francis. A. L. S. Folio. Philada., Jan. 4, 1779.

1441 Stanbury, Nathan. Colonial Judge. A. D. S. Small 4to. No date.

1442 Muhlenberg, Frederick A. Member of the Old Congress and Judge. D. S. 4to. Philada., Oct. 2, 1781.

1443 Shippen, Edw'd. Colonial Judge. A. L. S. 4to. Lancaster, Aug. 5, 1757.

1444 Shippen, Edw'd. Two D's. S., folio and 4to. Different dates. 2 pieces.
With fine impression of the enrollment officer of Lancaster County. 1774.

1445 Plumsted, Wm. Judge and Mayor of Philadelphia, 1750. Two A. D's. S. Different dates. 2 pieces.

1446 Peters, William. Judge of the Common Pleas. D. S. (four times). 2 pp. May 22, 1764.

1447 Ball, Wm. Judge of the Common Pleas. D. S. 4to. April 22, 1757. Also signed by Wm. Peters.

1448 Riddle, James. Judge of the High Court of Errors. A. L. S., 4to, Chambersburg, June 8, 1812, and A. L. S., folio, May 12, 1790. 2 pieces.

1449 Levy, Moses. Judge. Two A. L's. S., 4tos. Different dates. 2 pieces.

1450   Philadelphia Judges. A collection of documents and letters, by Rich'd Peters and others, relating to the permanent bridge on Market street, Philadelphia. 9 pieces.

1451   Philadelphia Judges. Jno. D. Coxe, Jno. Cadwalader, J. K. Kane, A. Randall, Rich'd Peters, Alex. Addison, C. S. Coxe, Jas. Riddle, Joel Jones, Moses Levy, R. G. White, Jno. Hallowell, E. D. Ingraham. A. L's. S. and D's. S., 4tos and folios. Various dates.   18 pieces.

1452   Philadelphia Judges. Joel Jones (Mayor), Geo. M. Dallas, J. I. Clarke Hare, Jos. Reed, Jas. Riddle, Timothy Matlack, J. B. Sutherland, J. Bouvier, Jos. Allison, W. N. Ashman, Craig Biddle, Thos. R. Elcock, J. K. Finletter, Wm. D. Hanna, Wm. D. Kelly, Jas. R. Ludlow, etc. A. L's. S. and D's. S., folios, 4tos and 8vos. Various dates.   43 pieces.

PENNSYLVANIA LAWYERS.

1453   Stevens, Thaddeus. The great commoner. A. L. S. May 4, 1838.

1454   Stevens, Thaddeus. A. L. S. 4to. Huntingdon, July 18, 1838.

1455   Bayard, John. Member of the Old Congress. A. D. S. 4to. Philadelphia, Sept. 23, 1780.

1456   Muhlenberg, Frederick A. Member of the Old Congress. D. S. 4to. Philadelphia, Sept. 26, 1783.

1457   Naylor, Chas. Governor of New Mexico—1847. A. L. S. 4to. Philadelphia, Aug. 20, 1831.

1458   Snyder, Simon. Governor of Pennsylvania. A. L. S. 4to. Lancaster, Feb. 13, 1801.

1459   Porter, David R. Governor of Pennsylvania. Two A. L's. S., 4tos. Different dates.   2 pieces.

1460   Shunk, Francis R. Governor of Pennsylvania. Two A. L's. S., 4tos. Different dates.   2 pieces.

1461   Bigler, Wm. Governor of Pennsylvania. A. L. S. 8vo. Feb. 28, 1866.

1462   Curtin, Andrew G. War Governor of Pennsylvania. A. L. S. 4to. 2 pp. Bellefonte, Aug. 16, 1843.

1463   Curtin, Andrew G. A. L. S. 8vo. No date.

1464   Hartranft, Jno. F. Governor of Pennsylvania. A. L. S. 4to. Harrisburg, May 13, 1876.

1465   Pennsylvania Lawyers. Jno. Moore, Henry A. Muhlenberg, F. Jordan, A. Breckenridge, Jas. H. Campbell, David Wilmot and others. A. L's. S. and D's. S., 4tos, folios and 8vos. Various dates.   32 pieces.

PHILADELPHIA LAWYERS.

1467   Wharton, Thos. J.   Legal writer.   Two A. L's. S., 4tos. Different dates.   2 pieces.

1468   Troubat, F. J.   Author of "Troubat and Haly's Practice." A. L. S.   4to.   Baltimore, Oct. 16, 1823.

1469   Tilghman, James.   Two A. L's. S., folio and 4to.   Different dates.   2 pieces.

1470   Tilghman, Edward.   Four A. L's. S., folios and 4tos. Various dates.   4 pieces.

1471   Swift, Chas.   A. L. S.   4to.   March 25, 1792.

1472   Sergeant, John.   Eight A. L's. S., 4tos.   Various dates.   8 pieces.

1473   Reed, Jos.   President of Pennsylvania.   D. S.   4to.   Sept. 6, 1779.

1474   Rawle, Wm.   Three A. L's. S. and one D. S., folios and 4tos.   Various dates.   4 pieces.

1475   Randall, Josiah.   Three A. L's. S., 4tos.   Various dates.   3 pieces.

1476   Purdon, John.   Author of " Purdon's Digest."   A. L. S. 4to.   April 27, 1835.

1477   Price, Eli K.   A. L. S. and A. D. S.   4tos.   Different dates.   2 pieces.

1478   Porter, J. M.   Secretary of War.   A. L. S.   4to.   Harrisburg, April 4, 1838.

1479   Pettit, Chas.   Member of the Old Congress.   A. L. S. 4to.   Philadelphia, Aug. 18, 1791.

1480   Peters, Rich'd, Jr.   The Reporter.   Three A. L's. S., 4tos and 8vos.   Various dates.   3 pieces.

1481   Naylor, Chas.   Governor of New Mexico.   A. L. S.   8vo. May 28, 1831.

1482   Morris, E. Joy.   Author.   A. L. S.   8vo.   Washington, Feb. 8, 1858.

1483   Miles, J.   The Reporter.   A. L. S.   8vo.   No date.

1484   Meredith, Wm.   Five A. L's. S., L's. S. and D's. S., 4tos, folios and 8vos.   Various dates.   5 pieces.

1485   Lewis, Wm.   Three A. L's. S., 4tos and folios.   Various dates.   3 pieces.

1486   Levy, Samson.   Two A. L's. S., 4tos.   Different dates.   2 pieces.

1487   Ingersoll, Jos. R.   Minister to England.   Four A. L's. S., 4tos and 8vos.   Various dates.   4 pieces.

1488 Ingersoll, Chas. J. Author of "History of the War of 1812." Four A. L's. S., 4tos. Various dates. 4 pieces.

1489 Howell, Rich'd. Governor of New Jersey. A. L. S. Folio. Trenton, Feb. 6, 1794.

1490 Hopkins, James. A. L. S. 4to. Dec. 21, 1789.

1491 Galloway, Joseph. Member of the Old Congress. "Denounced as a traitor on the floor of Congress." A. D. S. Folio. Jan. 21, 1763.

1492 Galloway, Joseph. A. D. S. Folio. 2 pp. Philadelphia, Aug. 3, 1769.

1493 Du Ponceau, Peter S. Two A. L's. S., 4tos. Different dates. 2 pieces.

1494 Duane, Wm. J. Secretary of the Treasury. Two A. L's. S., 8vo and 4to. Different dates. 2 pieces.

1495 Dallas, Geo. M. Vice-President. A. L. S. 4to. Jan. 7, 1819.

1496 Dallas, A. J. Secretary of the Treasury. Two A. D's. S. 4to and folio. Different dates. 2 pieces.

1497 Coxe, Tench. Member of the Old Congress. A. L. S. 4to. No date.

1498 Chew, Benj. Jr. Two A. L's. S. 8vos. Different dates. 2 pieces.

1499 Chauncey, Chas. Four A. L's. S. 4tos. Various dates. 4 pieces.

1500 Brown, David Paul. Three A. L's. S. 8vo and 4tos. 3 pieces.

1501 Binney, Horace. Two A. L's. S., and one A. D. S. 4tos and 8vo. Various dates. 3 pieces.

1502 Biddle, Nicholas. President of the U. S. Bank. Two A. L's. S., 4tos. Different dates. 2 pieces.

1503 Philadelphia Lawyers. A collection of sixty-six letters and documents, written by eminent Philadelphia lawyers. 4tos, folios and 8vos. 66 pieces.

1504 Pennsylvania Judges. A collection of sixty-one letters, written by eminent Pennsylvania judges, of the last twenty-five years. 8vos and 4tos. Various dates. 61 pieces.

1505 Vermont Judges, etc. Isaac F. Redfield, Jonathan H. Hubbard, Nathaniel Chipman, H. E. Stougton, etc. Fifty-three A. L's. S. and D's. S. 4tos and folios. Various dates. 53 pieces.

1506 Tennessee Judges, etc. A. Roane, Moses Fisk, Jos. Anderson, George W. Jones, Felix Robertson and others. Twenty-one A. L's. S. and D's. S. Folios and 4tos. Various dates. 21 pieces.

1507 Maine Judges, etc. Job Nelson, Samuel P. Benson, Erastus
      Foote, John Appleton, Ezekiel Whitman, W. P. Preble
      and others. Thirty-three A. L.'s. S. and D's. S. 4tos,
      folios and 8vos. Various dates. 33 pieces.

1508 Lousianna Judges, etc. Thos. J. Durant, E. K. Wilson, J. S.
      Whitaker, Thos. J. Summer, E. T. Merrick and others.
      Ten A. L's. S. 4tos and 8vos. Various dates. 10 pieces.

1509 Ohio Judges, etc. Joshua Collett, Elijah Hayward, Wm.
      Sprigg, B. Stover, Elisha Whittlesey and others.
      Eighty-four A. L's. S. and D's. S. Folios, 4tos and
      8vos. Various dates. 84 pieces.

1510 Texas Judges, etc. J. H. McLeary and others. Three
      A. L.'s. S. 4tos. Various dates. 3 pieces.

1511 Rhode Island Judges, etc. J. K. Angell, W. S. Burges,
      Tristram Burges, W. R. Staples, Dutee J. Pearce, John
      Knowles and others. Twenty-nine A. L's. S. 4tos and
      8vos. Various dates. 29 pieces.

1512 Arkansas Judges, etc. H. C. Caldwell, E. H. English,
      Townsend Dickerson and others. Thirteen A. L's. S.
      4tos and 8vos. Various dates. 13 pieces.

1513 Alabama Judges, etc. Benj. F. Porter, D. G. Logan, Thos.
      M. Peters and others. Thirty-three A. L's. S. 4tos and
      8vos. Various dates. 33 pieces.

1514 New Hamshire Judges, etc. Ichabod Goodwin, H. A.
      Cheney, C. Doe, J. A. Eastman and others. Forty-two
      A. L's. S. 8vos and 4tos. Various dates. 42 pieces.

1515 Colorado Judges, etc. A. J. Sampson and others. Six
      A. L's. S. 4tos. Various dates. 6 pieces.

1516 California Judges, etc. S. C. Hastings, Ogden Hoffman and
      others. Nine A. L's. S. 8vos and 4tos. Various dates.
      9 pieces.

1517 Indiana Judges, etc. A. G. Porter, J. T. McKinney, Jesse L.
      Holman, W. E. Niblack, D. P. Baldwin and others.
      Sixty-nine A. L's. S. 4tos and 8vos. Various dates.
      69 pieces.

1518 South Carolina Judges, etc. John Floyd, B. F. Dunkin, H.
      W. Desaussure, C. J. Colcock, Thos. Parker, D. E.
      Huges, Alex. Moultrie, Thos. Gaillard, Lewis Trezevant,
      E. Ramsey, J. f. Grimke, H. E. Pendleton, W. G. Mar-
      tin, David Graeme and others. Fifty-seven A. L's. S.
      and D's. S. Folios and 4tos. Various dates. 57 pieces.

1519 Judges of Western States and Territories. Granville G.
      Bennett, Samuel Maxwell, L. Crounse, Andrew J. Pop-
      pleton, John D. Hayes, E. D. Shattuck and others.
      Twenty-six A. L's. S. 8vos and 4tos. Various dates.
      26 pieces.

1520 Iowa Judges, etc. Charles Mason, C. C. Cole, John F. Dillon, Isaac Pendleton and others. Forty-four A. L's. S. 4tos and 8vos. Various dates.   44 pieces.

1521 Kansas Judges, etc. C. K. Gilchrist, W. C. Webb, R. J. Waters and others. Twenty-five A. L.'s. S. 4tos and 8vos. Various dates.   25 pieces.

1522 Kentucky Judges, etc. Thos. T. Davis, Caleb Wallace, Wm. Logan, John Trimble and others. Fifty-six A. L's. S. 4tos and folios. Various dates.   56 pieces.

1523 Illinois Judges, etc. Lyman Trumbull, M. D. Ewell, J. H. Bissel and others. Forty-seven A. L's. S. 4tos. Various dates.   47 pieces.

1524 North Corolina Judges, etc. Robert Strange, Duncan Cameron, A. Henderson and others. Sixteen A. L's. S. 4tos. Various dates.   16 pieces.

1525 Georgia Judges, etc. Robert M. Charlton, James Bullock, R. L. Gamble, Wm. C. Dawson and others. Thirty A. L's. S. and D's. S. 4tos and folios. Various dates.   30 pieces.

1526 Florida Judges, etc. W. Archer Cocke, J. H. Bronson and others. Ten A. L's. S. 8vos and 4tos. Various dates.   10 pieces.

1527 District of Columbia Judges, etc. W. Cranch, Charles C. Nott, John A. Bowles and others. Eighteen A. L's. S. 4tos and 8vos. Various dates.   18 pieces.

1528 Delaware Judges, etc. Jacob Moore, A. B. Love, Isaac Davis, Willard Hall, George Read and others. Thirty A. L's. S. and I.'s. S. Folios, 4tos and 8vos. Various dates.   30 pieces.

1529 Maryland Judges, etc. A. W. Bateman, Oliver Miller, H. Stockbridge, D. Weisel, Thomas F. Bowie, John Ridout, Thomas Jennings and others. Fity-seven A. L's. S. and D's. S. Folios, 4tos and 8vos. Various dates.   57 pieces.

1530 Virginia and West Virginia Judges, etc. Richard Parker, George A. Hay, G. K. Taylor, William Nelson and others. Fifty-eight A. L's. S. 4tos and 8vos. Various dates. 58 pieces.

1531 Wisconsin Judges, etc. A. G. Miller, L. S. Dixon, E. Ellwell and others. Eleven A. L's. S. 4tos and 8vos. Various dates.   11 pieces.

1532 New Jersey Judges and Judges of other States, Arthur Livermore, Sam'l A. Talcott, J. Rutledge, Isaac Smith, Wm. Halsey, Jos. C. Hornblower and others. One hundred and twelve A. L's. S., L's. S. and D's. S. Folios, 4tos and 8vos. Various dates.   112 pieces.

1533 Michigan Judges, etc. Ross Wilkins, E. H. Wilson, T. M. Cooley, N. R. Ramsdell, Chas. Upson and others. Thirty-four A. L's. S. 4tos and 8vos. Various dates. 34 pieces.

1534 Mississippi Judges, etc. Chas. Scott, Alex. M. Clayton, Wm. G. Harris, T. A. Marshall and others. Fourteen A. L's. S. 4tos and 8vos. Various dates. 14 pieces.

1535 Missouri Judges, etc. Jno. C. Edwards, Beverley Tucker, David Wagner, C. C. Whittlesey and others. Thirty A. L's. S. 8vos and 4tos. Various dates. 30 pieces.

1536 Minnesota Judges, etc. Isaac Atwater, Thos. Wilson and others. Sixteen A. L's. S. 8vos and 4tos. Various dates. 16 pieces.

1537 New York Judges, etc. R. M. Blatchford, Reuben H. Walwroth, Erastus Root, D. Hoffman, Ezekiel Cowen, Sam'l Beardsley, Wm. B. Bears, Rich'd Harrison and others. One hundred and eighty-two A. L's. S. and D's. S. Folios, 4tos and 8vos. Various dates. 182 pieces.

1538 Judges of different States. Jos. C. Hornblower, Francis S. Nevins, Caleb S. Green, Gabriel H. Ford, L. Q. C. Elmer, John Chetwood, B. Williamson, A. O. Zabriskie, H. H. Leavitt, Wm. Lawrence, Rich'd Parker and others. Fifty A. L's. S. 4tos and 8vos. Various dates. 50 pieces.

1539 Judges of different States. John J. Allen, Creed Taylor, John T. Lomax, John Coulter, Thos. L. Lee, P. Carrington, Nicholas Thomas, R. R. Reid, S. R. Mallory, J. Cuyler, Geo. W. Crawford, Jno. Milledge, Herschel V. Johnson, Jas. W. Jackson, R. H. Wilde, Thos. W. Cobb, M. J. Crawford, D. A. Walker, John Erskine and others. Fifty A. L's. S. 4tos and 8vos. Various dates. 50 pieces.

1540 Judges of different States. H. G. Burton, Thos. Bragg, Jno. W. Daniel, Jno. K. Hackett, T. A. Howard, K. S. Bingham, Chas. Upshur, Wm. L. Stoughton, T. M. Cooley, D. M. Bates, Jos. W. Chalmers, W. L. Sharkey, W. S. Holman, Isaac Blackford, W. E. Niblack, Isaac F. Redfield, Milo L. Bennett, A. B. Meek and others. Forty-seven A. L's. S. 4tos and 8vos. Various dates. 47 pieces.

1541 Judges of different States. H. W. Hilliard, A. B. Meek, B. F. Rice, Thos. P. Eskridge, Jas. B. McKean, H. W. Corbett, Thos. P. Hawley, P. P. Prim, Moses Hallett, Jno. F. Dillon, Jos. Brevard, W. Thompson, Hugh Rutledge, Jno. J. Pringle, E. R. Potter, Geo. Eustis, Sam'l D. Bell, Dan'l Clark, Wm. L. Foster, Horatio Rogers, Jno. Appleton, Geo. Evans and others. Thirty-six A. L's. S. 4tos and 8vos. Various dates. 36 pieces.

Compound Division

Q What is compound Division

A When several numbers of Divers Denomination
are given to be divided by 1 common divisor this called
Compound Division

$$
\begin{array}{l}
\pounds \quad S \quad D \\
2)48 - 12 - 6\tfrac{1}{2} \\
24 - 6 - 3\tfrac{3}{4} \\
2 \\
\hline
48 - 12 - 6\tfrac{1}{2}
\end{array}
\qquad
\begin{array}{l}
\ell b \quad oz \quad dr \\
7)46 - 12 - 113 \\
9 - 5 - 113 \\
5 \\
\hline
46 \quad 12 - 10
\end{array}
$$

1533 Michigan Judges, etc. Ross Wilkins, E. H. Wilson, T. M. Cooley, N. R. Ramsdell, Chas. Upson and others. Thirty-four A. L's. S. 4tos and 8vos. Various dates.
34 pieces.

1534 Mississippi Judges, etc. Chas. Scott, Alex. M. Clayton, Wm. G. Harris, T. A. Marshall and others. Fourteen A. L's. S. 4tos and 8vos. Various dates. 14 pieces.

1535 Missouri Judges, etc. Jno. C. Edwards, Beverley Tucker, David Wagner, C. C. Whittlesey and others. Thirty A. L's. S. 8vos and 4tos. Various dates. 30 pieces.

1536 Minnesota Judges, etc. Isaac Atwater, Thos. Wilson and others. Sixteen A. L's. S. 8vos and 4tos. Various dates. 16 pieces.

1537 New York Judges, etc. R. M. Blatchford, Reuben H. Walwroth, Erastus Root, D. Hoffman, Ezekiel Cowen, Sam'l Beardsley, Wm. B. Bears, Rich'd Harrison and others. One hundred and eighty-two A. L's. S. and D's. S. Folios, 4tos and 8vos. Various dates. 182 pieces.

1538 Judges of different States. Jos. C. Hornblower, Francis S. Nevins, Caleb S. Green, Gabriel H. Ford, L. Q. C. Elmer, John Chetwood, B. Williamson, A. O. Zabriskie, H. H. Leavitt, Wm. Lawrence, Rich'd Parker and others. Fifty A. L's. S. 4tos and 8vos. Various dates. 50 pieces.

1539 Judges of different States. John J. Allen, Creed Taylor, John T. Lomax, John Coulter, Thos. L. Lee, P. Carrington, Nicholas Thomas, R. R. Reid, S. R. Mallory, J. Cuyler, Geo. W. Crawford, Jno. Milledge, Herschel V. Johnson, Jas. W. Jackson, R. H. Wilde, Thos. W. Cobb, M. J. Crawford, D. A. Walker, John Erskine and others. Fifty A. L's. S. 4tos and 8vos. Various dates.
50 pieces.

1540 Judges of different States. H. G. Burton, Thos. Bragg, Jno. W. Daniel, Jno. K. Hackett, T. A. Howard, K. S. Bingham, Chas. Upshur, Wm. L. Stoughton, T. M. Cooley, D. M. Bates, Jos. W. Chalmers, W. L. Sharkey, W. S. Holman, Isaac Blackford, W. E. Niblack, Isaac F. Redfield, Milo L. Bennett, A. B. Meek and others. Forty-seven A. L's. S. 4tos and 8vos. Various dates.
47 pieces.

1541 Judges of different States. H. W. Hilliard, A. B. Meek, B. F. Rice, Thos. P. Eskridge, Jas. B. McKean, H. W. Corbett, Thos. P. Hawley, P. P. Prim, Moses Hallett, Jno. F. Dillon, Jos. Brevard, W. Thompson, Hugh Rutledge, Jno. J. Pringle, E. R. Potter, Geo. Eustis, Sam'l D. Bell, Dan'l Clark, Wm. L. Foster, Horatio Rogers, Jno. Appleton, Geo. Evans and others. Thirty-six A. L's. S. 4tos and 8vos. Various dates. 36 pieces.

To Exercise Multiplication

There were 40 men concern'd in payment
a sum of money, and each man paid 12 £ 14 s
how much was paid in all —

$$\begin{array}{r} 12\text{-}14 \\ 40 \\ \hline 508\text{-}0 \\ 12)\,f \end{array}$$

If 1 foot contain 12 inches I demand how their
are in 126 feet:—

$$\begin{array}{r} 126 \\ 12 \\ \hline 252 \\ 126 \\ \hline 12)1512 \\ 126 \end{array}$$

Of Compound Division

Q What is compound Division

A When several numbers of Divers Denomination
are given to be divided by common divisor this ealld
compound Division

$$\begin{array}{lll}
& \pounds\ s\ D & lb\ oz\ dr \\
24)8\text{-}12\text{-}6\tfrac{1}{4} & 9)9\text{-}12\text{-}14\tfrac{3}{3} \\
12)\text{-}6\text{-}3\tfrac{1}{4} & 9\text{-}3\text{-}\tfrac{5}{5} \\
\hline
48\text{-}12\text{-}6\tfrac{1}{4} & 76\ 12\text{-}10
\end{array}$$

Abraham Lincoln His Book

Compound Multiplication

Q What is Compound Multiplication
A When several numbers of divers Denomination
are given to be multiplied by one Common multiplier
this is called Compound multiplication

10000
27
70000
20000
27
0000

Lincoln Memorial Collection.

Letters and Documents, Etc., Written by Abraham Lincoln; Law Books and Furniture From His Office and Furniture From His Residence, in Springfield, Illinois.

1542 Lincoln, Abraham.   Autograph Letter, signed.   4to.
New Salem, November 10, 1835. To George Duncan,
Governor of Illinois.   With address.

> Written at the time Lincoln was postmaster at New Salem, Ill. A
> very early and fine specimen.

1543 Lincoln, Abraham.   Autograph Letter, signed.   8vo.
Executive Mansion, June 24, 1861. To the Secretary
of State.

> Fine specimen, written in the first year of his presidency, calling for
> a cabinet meeting.

1544 Lincoln, Abraham.   Autograph Note, signed, on a visiting
card.   August 18, 1863.

> "Sec. of the Treasury, please see this Lady who says she is the wife
> of a preacher who is in the war as a Captain in the 126th N. Y. She
> wants employment.
> "Aug. 18, 1863.   A. LINCOLN."
>
> This note is characteristic of the great man. Mrs. General Winfield
> Scott had evidently just left her card, and when this poor woman
> applied for a position, no paper being handy, Lincoln picked up Mrs.
> Scott's visiting card and wrote the above short note to the Secretary of
> the Treasury on the back of it.

1545 Lincoln, Abraham.   Autograph Letter, signed.   8vo.
Washington, February 3, 1862. To his law partner,
William H. Herndon.

> "DEAR WILLIAM.
>
> "Yours of January 30th is just received. Do just as you say
> about the money matters, as you well know, I have not time to write a
> letter of respectable length.   God bless you, says
>   "your friend
>   "A. LINCOLN."

1546 Lincoln, Abraham.   Autograph Letter, signed.   4to.
Pekin, Illinois, October 3, 1853. To M. Brayman.
With address.

> "Neither the county of McLean nor any on one its behalf has yet
> made engagements with me in relation to its suit with the Illinois Cen-
> tral Railroad, on the subject of taxation. I am now free to make an
> engagement for the Road and if you think fit you may ' count me in.'
> Please write me on receipt of this." Etc., etc.

Compound Multiplication

Q. What is Compound Multiplication? A. When several numbers of divers Denominations are given to be multiplied by one common multiplier, then is called Compound Multiplication.

£ s D
17 - 3 - 1½
       2
25·7 - 6 - 2¾
17 - 3 1½

lb - oz - dwt gr
17 - 5 - 12 - 16
           3
35·2 - 7 - 12 - 4
17 - 3 - 12 - 4

56 7 at 7 Cwts
      9
27/08

45 6 9 at 9 Cwts

134 36 at 8968 R.Band
      89
5 888 4

Bonds at 9 Shillings

£ - s - d
6 - 4 - 9 - 7
          2¾
35 - 7 - 8 - 4
129 - 2 - 8
168 - 0 - 6 - 4

O. An army of a 10000 men having plundered a City took so much money that when it was shared among them each man had (as 27, 9 done) how much among us Taken in all

10000
   27
70000
20000
2700000000000
2 7 0 0 0 0

1 / 7
4 / 8
2 11·

Lincoln Memorial Collection.

Letters and Documents, Etc., Written by Abraham Lincoln; Law Books and Furniture From His Office and Furniture From His Residence, in Springfield, Illinois.

1542 Lincoln, Abraham. Autograph Letter, signed. 4to. New Salem, November 10, 1835. To George Duncan, Governor of Illinois. With address.

> Written at the time Lincoln was postmaster at New Salem, Ill. A very early and fine specimen.

1543 Lincoln, Abraham. Autograph Letter, signed. 8vo. Executive Mansion, June 24, 1861. To the Secretary of State.

> Fine specimen, written in the first year of his presidency, calling for a cabinet meeting.

1544 Lincoln, Abraham. Autograph Note, signed, on a visiting card. August 18, 1863.

> "Sec. of the Treasury, please see this Lady who says she is the wife of a preacher who is in the war as a Captain in the 126th N. Y. She wants employment.
> "Aug. 18, 1863.   A. Lincoln."
>
> This note is characteristic of the great man. Mrs. General Winfield Scott had evidently just left her card, and when this poor woman applied for a position, no paper being handy, Lincoln picked up Mrs. Scott's visiting card and wrote the above short note to the Secretary of the Treasury on the back of it.

1545 Lincoln, Abraham. Autograph Letter, signed. 8vo. Washington, February 3, 1862. To his law partner, William H. Herndon.

> "Dear William.
>
> "Yours of January 30th is just received. Do just as you say about the money matters, as you well know, I have not time to write a letter of respectable length.   God bless you, says
> "your friend
> "A. Lincoln."

1546 Lincoln, Abraham. Autograph Letter, signed. 4to. Pekin, Illinois, October 3, 1853. To M. Brayman. With address.

> "Neither the county of McLean nor any on one its behalf has yet made engagements with me in relation to its suit with the Illinois Central Railroad, on the subject of taxation. I am now free to make an engagement for the Road and if you think fit you may ' count me in.' Please write me on receipt of this."   Etc., etc.

1547　Lincoln, Abraham.　Autograph Document, signed.　Folio. (About 1856).

Lincoln's autograph copy of his bill for legal services rendered the Illinois Central Railroad Company in suit decided in the Supreme Court in the State of Illinois, December, 1855. Amount of bill, $5000, to which Lincoln has appended the names of six members of the Illinois bar, who certify to the amount not being unreasonable—Grant Goodrich, N. B. Judd, Archibald Williams, N. H. Purple, O. H. Browning and R. S. Blackwell.

1548　Lincoln, Abraham.　Document, signed.　Small 4to. Chicago, October 7, 1853.

A check for $250 given by Mr. Brayman to Abraham Lincoln as a retainer, with the understanding that when the suit—McLean County vs. Illinois Central R. R. Co—for county taxes was decided he should receive $1000 more. Mr. Lincoln spent much time and labor on the case, and argued it twice before the Illinois Supreme Court, and finally winning it in December, 1855. Lincoln came to Chicago to collect his fee. Mr. Brayman was absent at the time, and the bill was presented to the superintendent. He refused to authorize the payment of the bill on the ground that it was excessive, remarking "that it was as much as a first-class lawyer would have charged." Mr. Lincoln then brought suit for $5000, less the $250 retainer. Six leading lawyers of Illinois certified that, considering the great interests at stake and the valuable points gained for the company, the charge was reasonable. Mr. Lincoln won the suit, and the company paid the bill. About ten years afterward this superintendent was nominated by the Democratic party for the presidency of the United States, and was defeated by Mr. Lincoln by more than a million majority. The railroad superintendent was Gen. Geo. B. McClellan.

Lots 1546, 1547 and 1548 should not be separated, as they form a very interesting bit of history.

1549　Lincoln, Abraham.　A leaf from his Exercise Book.　In autograph, whereon he has written his name.　Folio.

The facsimile, which accompanies this catalogue, will better describe this interesting relic of the boyhood days of the great and good man more than any elaboration from my pen.

1550　Lincoln, Abraham.　Autograph Document, signed (twice). Folio.　2 pp.　April 5, 1856.

Brief, written by Lincoln, June 18, 1853, in the case of Remington K. Webster vs. George A. Rhodes and George M. Angell.

1551　Lincoln, Abraham.　Autograph Notes of a case.　Folio. 2 pp.　(About 1856-7).

1552　Lincoln, Abraham.　Autograph Document, signed.　Folio.

Preparation for trial in the case of Leonard H. Wilkey vs. Benjamin S. Prettyman.　(Written about 1856-7).

1553　Lincoln, Abraham.　Autograph Document, signed Logan, Stuart & Lincoln.　Folio.　May 26, 1837.

An agreement made by Mary Anderson and Richard Anderson with the firm of Logan, Stuart & Lincoln to recover certain lands on a conditional fee of one-half of the land. All in the handwriting of Abraham Lincoln.

1554   Lincoln, Abraham. Autograph Document, 4to, 1836, and
Autograph Document, 4to, June 17, 1843.   2 pieces.

    The former is of notes of a survey, made by Lincoln, of twelve
acres of land in Rock Creek, Menard County, Illinois, in 1836, and
the latter is a legal document.

1555   Lincoln, Abraham. Autograph Document. Folio. 1858.

    Instructions to United States Marshal to levy on certain described
lands to satisfy two judgments obtained by S. C. Davis & Co.

1556   Lincoln, Abraham. Autograph Memorandum. Small 4to.

    A scrap of paper evidently used by the great statesman to tie on top
of a bundle of law papers. On this Lincoln has written : " When you
can't find *it* anywhere, look into this."

1557   Lincoln, Abraham.   Autograph   Documents, signed.
(Stuart & Lincoln). 1836 to 1838. Small 4tos. 13 pieces.

    Thirteen bills for services rendered by the firm of Stuart & Lincoln.
All in Lincoln's handwriting.

1558   Lincoln, Abraham. Autograph Document. Folio. June
· 1, 1858.

    Paper in chancery suit of James A. Barrett *vs.* heirs and others of
William McDonald and James Kizer.

1559   Lincoln, Abraham. Autograph Document, signed. (Abraham Lincoln). Folio. April 20, 1838.

    An agreement made by James W. Crain with John T. Stuart and
Abraham Lincoln to prosecute a suit for the recovery of land, on a conditional fee of $500.

1560   Lincoln, Abraham. Autograph Document. Folio. About
1857.

    Tracing of chain of title to a piece of real estate in Logan County,
Illinois.

1561   Lincoln, Abraham. Autograph Document, signed. Folio.
2 pages. April 6, 1856.

    Settlement of the case of Remington K. Webster *vs.* George M.
Angell and George A. Rhodes, by arbitration.

1562   Lincoln, Abraham. Autograph Document, signed (and
with signature, in full, in the body). Folio. October
23, 1847.

    Lease written by Lincoln, when he rented his home in Springfield,
during the time he was in Congress. Leased first by Christopher Lud-
lam, and afterwards to Mason Brayman.

1563   Lincoln, Abraham. Autograph Document. Folio. About
1858.

    Preparation for lawsuit.

1564   Lincoln, Abraham. Autograph Memoranda. Folio. 6
pages. About 1850.

    Lincoln's docket of thirty-eight cases, written by himself in 1850.

1565 Lincoln, Abraham. Autograph Memoranda. Folio. 3 pages. 1850.

Notes made by Lincoln in the trial of Moses Loe, for murder, in 1850. Exceedingly interesting.

1566 Lincoln, Abraham. Autograph Memoranda. Folio. (About 1857).

Memoranda of lawsuits.

1567 Lincoln, Abraham. Autograph Memoranda. Folio. (About 1856).

Notes on the taxing of the McLean County Bank, in the suit of McLean County Bank vs. City of Bloomington.

1568 Lincoln, Abraham. Autograph Document. 4to. 3 pages. (About 1850).

Chancery bill in the Circuit Court of the United States.

1569 Lincoln, Abraham. Autograph Document. Folio. About 1845.

Notes on abstract of title to real estate.

1570 Lincoln, Abraham. Autograph Indorsement, signed. April 15, 1862.

Indorsement on a letter regarding ordnance supplies.

1571 Lincoln, Abraham. The original fee-book of the firm of Lincoln & Herndon, for the year 1847. 4to. 36 pages.

This book is a very interesting memento of the good man's early career as a lawyer. The moderate charges attached to the various entries show the modesty of the man and his underestimate of the value of his legal services.

1572 Lincoln, Mrs. Abraham. The wife of President Lincoln. Autograph Letter, signed. 4to. Chicago, April 6 (no year). To O. S. Halsted.

1573 Lincoln, Abraham. The dispatch sent by Abraham Lincoln to William H. Herndon, dated February 19, 1863.

This is the original dispatch, as delivered by the Illinois and Mississippi Telegraph Company, from Lincoln to his law partner, and reads: " Would you accept a job of about a month's duration at St. Louis, five dollars a day and mileage? Answer. A. LINCOLN."

Also the original addressed envelope, and an autograph letter, signed, of William H. Herndon, in which he says: "It was distinctly understood between Lincoln and myself that I wanted to hold no office under his administration, as I held the Bank Commissioner's office under Gov. Bissel, who appointed me at the solicitation and request of Mr. Lincoln."

1574 Lincoln's Teacher. Autograph Letter, signed, of D. F. Hanks, Abraham Lincoln's teacher. Dated February 1, 1866.

The spelling of this letter and the grammatical construction portray the limited knowledge that was simply necessary, in the early pioneer days of the West, for a man to have in order, to fill the position of schoolmaster, and gives incontestable proof that, with such a teacher, Lincoln must have been a self-made man.

1575   Lincoln, Abraham. A dispatch sent by Abraham Lincoln to Jesse K. DuBois at Springfield, Illinois, July 11, 1863, soon after the battle of Gettysburg.

"WASHINGTON, July 11th, 9.10 A.M.

"*To Hon. Jesse K. DuBois, Springfield:*

"It is certain that after three days fighting at Gettysburg, Lee withdrew and made for the Potomac. That he found the river so swollen as to prevent his crossing; that he is still this side near Hagerstown and Williamsport preparing to defend himself, and that Meade is close upon him preparing to attack him, heavy skirmishing having occurred nearly all day yesterday. I am more than satisfied with what has happened north of the Potomac, so far, and am anxious and hopeful for what is to come. "A. LINCOLN,

"*Pres't. U. S.*"

Together with the letter from Lincoln DuBois mentioning the fact that this dispatch was found among his late father's papers.

1576   Lincoln, Abraham. Duplicate of his marriage license, filled in, in the handwriting of Abraham Lincoln. Issued by M. W. Weatherby, clerk of the county court, Springfield, Illinois, November 4, 1842. 4to.

This is the certificate of the marriage of Abraham Lincoln to Mary Todd; contains Lincoln's name in full, and is signed by Rev. Charles Dresser, the clergyman who performed the marriage ceremony. Presented to the owner by Mrs. W. H. Herndon.

1577   Lincoln, Abraham. A piece of the outside casket which inclosed the remains of Abraham Lincoln.

This was obtained at the time of the dedication of the National Lincoln Monument in 1874, there being present members of the Monument Association, among whom was the Vice-President, the Hon. Jesse K. DuBois, to whom this was given as a memento. The casket was opened and the remains viewed and declared to be those of Mr. Lincoln. Accompanied with a certificate of genuineness, signed by Lincoln DuBois, son of the Hon. Jesse K. DuBois.

1578   Lincoln, Abraham. Frame, containing a silver star and pieces of satin, crape, velvet and silver braid, which were on the dais on the catafalque on which rested the remains of Abraham Lincoln, in the Hall of Representatives at Springfield, Illinois, May 3, 1865. Here was exposed for the last time the face so dear to the nation, and here was the end of the greatest mourning procession which the world had ever beheld.

Accompanied with an affidavit of John R. Campbell, of Springfield, Illinois, who took them from the dais and the catafalque above mentioned.

LINCOLN'S LAW BOOKS.

1579　A volume containing the Declaration of Independence, Constitution of the United States, the first constitution of the State of Indiana, and various acts passed by its State legislature during the session of 1823–24.　8vo, boards.

This book, although in a dilapidated form, wanting title-page and several leaves at end, was the first law book that Lincoln ever used, and is accompanied with an autograph letter signed by Wm. H. Herndon, his law partner, as to its authenticity.

1580　Chitty's Treatise On Pleading and Parties To Action. 3 vols.　8vo, sheep.　Springfield, Massachusetts, 1844.

Firm name in each volume—Lincoln & Herndon. (Binding broken).

1581　Stephen's Commentaries on the Laws of England. 4 vols.　8vo, sheep.　New York, 1841.

Firm name of Lincoln & Herndon in each volume.

1582　Greenleaf on the Law of Evidence.　Vol. I.　8vo, sheep. Boston, 1848.　(Binding broken).

1583　Revised Statutes of the State of Illinois.　8vo, sheep. Springfield, Massachusetts, 1844.

Firm name of Lincoln & Herndon on inside of cover.

1584　Kent's Commentaries on American Law.　4 vols.　8vo, sheep.　New York, 1851.

Firm name of Lincoln & Herndon in each volume. (Binding broken).

1585　Smith's Law of Landlord and Tenant.　8vo, sheep.　Philadelphia, 1856.

Firm name of Lincoln & Herndon inside of cover.

1586　Story's Commentaries on Equity Jurisprudence.　2 vols. 8vo, sheep.　Boston, 1843.

Firm name of Lincoln & Herndon in each volume in the handwriting of Abraham Lincoln.

1587　Parson's Law of Contract.　2 vols.　8vo, sheep.　Boston, 1851.

Firm name of Lincoln & Herndon in each volume.

1588　Wharton's Treatise on Criminal Law.　8vo, sheep.　Philadelphia, 1857.

Firm name of Lincoln & Herndon on inside of cover.

1589　Redfield's Treatise Upon the Law of Railways.　8vo. sheep.　Boston, 1858.

Firm name of Lincoln & Herndon on inside of cover.

1590　Stephen's Treatise on the Principles of Pleading.　8vo, sheep.　Philadelphia, 1857.

Fine name of Lincoln and Herndon on the inside of cover.

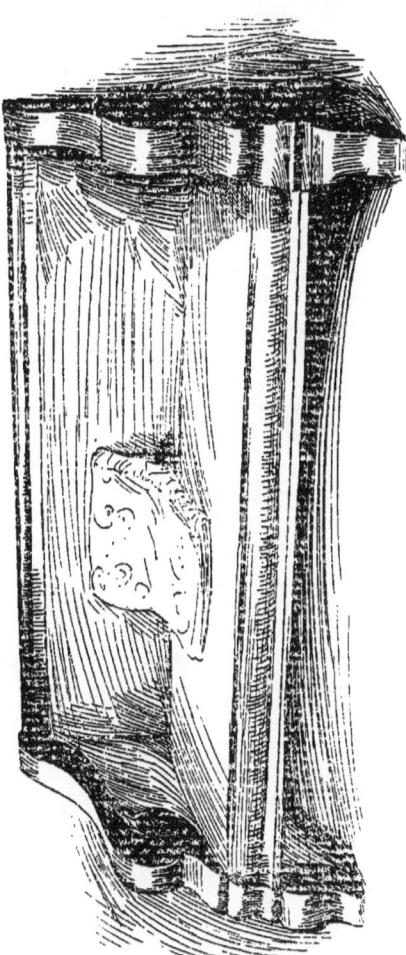

No. 1591.

THE SOFA MADE TO ORDER OF ABRAHAM LINCOLN.

No. 1502.

ANTIQUE MAHOGANY TABLE FROM LINCOLN'S PARLOR.

LINCOLN'S FURNITURE.

1591   Antique Mahogany Haircloth Sofa.

    This old mahogany veneered sofa was made by hand, at Springfield, by Daniel E. Ruckel, in 1837, for Mr. Lincoln, on his order, and used by Mr. Lincoln until February, 1861. Purchased from J. E. Roll, a resident of Springfield, who had known Mr. Lincoln since 1831. When Mr. Roll turned this memento over to Mr. Keyes, he wrote a letter explaining why he had originally been anxious to obtain possession of it. In that letter he says:—"I became acquainted with Abraham Lincoln in February, 1831, having been employed to assist him in building the second flatboat ever constructed on the Sangamon river, or in the State of Illinois, earning by that labor about 30 cents a day. (The first flatboat built sunk soon after being launched from her moorings). Mr. Lincoln was employed at that time by Mr. Offutt at a salary of $15 a month, which at that time was considered good wages for a mechanic. After Mr. Lincoln completed the boat I accompanied him as far down the river as Lemon's bend, where I bade him ' good-by,' he going on to New Orleans, where he sold the boat and the cargo. Mr. Lincoln returned to Illinois and settled in New Salem, Menard county. We were friends up to the time of his death, and I bought the sofa as a keepsake, knowing that it was made especially for him on his order, as he was unable to find one long enough for his use already manufactured."

    Accompanied by the affidavits of Jacob Ruckel, testifying that he upholstered and sold the sofa to Lincoln in 1837; of John E. Roll as to its authenticity, and of Alfred A. Worth, a justice of the peace, in regard to the deponent's character.

1592   An Antique Mahogany Side Table, with white marble top. (Marble broken).

1593   Large French-plate Mirror, gilt frame.

1594 to 1599   Six Antique Mahogany Chairs, with tufted haircloth seats.

1600   Large Axminster Rug.

    Lots 1592 to 1600 formed a portion of the furnishing of Abraham Lincoln's parlor, and were obtained from Mr. Allen Miller, who bought them from Mr. and Mrs. Lincoln, in February, 1861. As Mr. Miller was about to take them from the Lincoln residence, Mr. Lincoln requested that the table and one of the chairs remain, as he had some very important writing that he must attend to before leaving Springfield. Consequently, the very last writing that Mr. Lincoln did before leaving Illinois was upon this identical table and seated in one of these chairs.

    Accompanied with the affidavit of the Miller family as to genuineness.

1601　The Old Hickory Chair in which Mr. Lincoln was sitting when he received the dispatch announcing his nomination for the presidency.

Presented to the collection by the *Illinois State Journal*, of Springfield, Ill. It is made of hickory withes, with a hoop-pole seat, and was for years used as the repository for exchanges in the office of the Springfield *Journal*. No matter who or what was in that chair when Lincoln dropped into gossip, he had to have that seat. On May 13, 1886, J. R. Stewart, editor of the *Journal*, sent the chair to Mr. Keyes, with a letter, in which he said : " The publishers of the *Journal*, having their attention called to the collection of Lincoln mementos which you are gathering, authorize me, as a means of properly rounding out the lot, to present to you the old rustic chair which has faithfully held exchanges in this office for many years, but which is now too weak in the joints to do any other service unless repaired. It is the chair in which Abraham Lincoln was sitting when he received from Chicago the dispatch announcing his first nomination for the presidency. We shall be happy if you can find some man to sit in it who is anywhere near as great as Lincoln was."

Accompanied by affidavit of J. R. Stewart, editor of the *Illinois State Journal*, as to its genuineness.

1602　Mahogany Bureau, from the bedroom of Abraham Lincoln.

Purchased by E. Figueri from Mr. and Mrs. Lincoln, in 1861. Sold to John C. Barker, May 26, 1865. Purchased for the collection from the surviving members of John C. Barker's family.

Accompanied with Figueri's affidavit as to its genuineness.

1603　Antique Mahogany Worktable, with pedestal base and two drawers. Owned by Abraham Lincoln.

1604　Antique Walnut Tête-à-tête Table. Owned by Abraham Lincoln.

The above two last items were purchased from Mr. and Mrs. Lincoln by their neighbor, J. M. Forder, just before their removal to Washington, in 1861, and remained in Mr. Forder's possesion till purchased by the Lincoln Memorial Collection Association.

Accompanied by J. M. Forder's affidavit as to their genuineness.

1605　Walnut Table, from the bedroom of Abraham Lincoln.

Evidently used as a washhand stand. Purchased by E. Figueri from Mr. and Mrs. Lincoln, in 1861. See affidavit with lot 1602.

1606　Carriage Cushion used by Abraham Lincoln and family.

Presented to the " Lincoln Memorial Collection " by Major Alfred A. North, of Springfield, Ill.

No, 1601.

OLD HICKORY CHAIR IN WHICH LINCOLN WAS SITTING
WHEN HE RECEIVED THE DISPATCH ANNOUNCING HIS
NOMINATION FOR THE PRESIDENCY.

No. 1603.

MAHOGANY WORKTABLE FROM
LINCOLN'S PARLOR.

No. 1594.

ONE OF THE SIX CHAIRS FROM
LINCOLN'S PARLOR.

1607   Old-fashioned Split-bottom Chair. Repaired for Caleb
Carman by Abraham Lincoln.

> With affidavit, to wit :—
>
> "Caleb Carman, being duly sworn, deposes that the chair which is
> this day sold to the Lincoln Memorial Collection of Chicago, is the
> same chair which Abraham Lincoln repaired for me, putting in this
> identical bottom or seat which is now in the chair, at the time he was
> boarding with me at New Salem, Illinois, about the year 1835.
>
> "For over fifty years this chair has been in my house.
>
>   "CALEB CARMEN. [SEAL]
>
> "Subscribed and sworn before me, this twentieth day of May, A. D.
> 1887.   A. W. McGRACKIN,
>   { Seal County Court, }   "County Clerk."
>   { Menard Co., Ill. }

1608   Walnut Office Table, or Desk, used by Abraham Lincoln
in his law office.

1609   Walnut Double-door Bookcase, which rested on the office
table used by Abraham Lincoln in his law office.

1610   Walnut Skeleton Bookcase used by Abraham Lincoln in
his law office.

1611   Large, Round, Wooden Inkstand used by Abraham Lincoln.

> Of the inkstand his law partner writes (in a letter which accompanies
> it) : "This inkstand was the property of Abraham Lincoln, and was
> kept in his office for years; and out of which he wrote 'The-house-
> divided-against-itself' speech which caused much discussion, as to its
> propriety, in the Republican ranks of that day. Douglas attacked it
> with energy, ability and vehemence, but it still lives."
>
> Lots 1608, 1609, 1610 and 1611 are fully authenticated by letters of
> Mr. W. H. Herndon, Lincoln's law partner.

1612   Walnut Double-door Cupboard, from Abraham Lincoln's
house.

> Purchased from Mr. and Mrs. Abraham Lincoln by Allen Miller, in
> February, 1861, and accompanied with affidavit as to its genuineness.

1613   Portrait of Abraham Lincoln.

> Large cabinet photograph of Abraham Lincoln, taken in 1857, and
> used during the celebrated campaign between Lincoln and Douglas.
> This is the original photograph which was presented by Mr. Lincoln to
> Major Alfred North, of Springfield, Ill., remaining in his possession
> twenty-nine years, when he presented it to the Lincoln Memorial
> Collection, of Chicago, May, 1886.

1614   Oil Portrait of Abraham Lincoln.   Life-size; three-quarter
       length.   Painted by A. E. Darling, of Springfield, Ill.
       In gilt frame.

       Belonged to General Mason Brayman, Lincoln's neighbor and friend.
       In a letter which accompanies the portrait General Brayman says:—

       "The life-size oil portrait of Abraham Lincoln, which I to-day deliver
       to you, was painted by the artist A. E. Darling, after Mr. Lincoln's
       election—not before, as is shown by the fact that the whiskers were
       grown after that event." * * * * "Soon after Mr. Lincoln's
       death I purchased the picture of Mr. Darling, who resided in Springfield,
       for $800, and it has remained in my possession till now, nearly the
       whole time the chief attraction of my parlor. I prized it for its admirable
       fidelity, knowing Mr. L. intimately; of hundreds who came to see—all
       agreed with me on that point." Etc.

1615   Oil Portrait of Abraham Lincoln.   Life size, half length.
       Painted by M. Yamasaki, 1886.   In gilt frame.

1616   Lincoln, Abraham.   Notes of a survey made in 1836.
       4to.   Together with a photograph of a letter written
       by A. Lincoln to A. Campbell in 1858.

1617   Facsimile of the Emancipation Proclamation.   Litho-
       graphed by E. Mendel, Chicago, 1863.   In oak frame.

1618   Facsimile of the Declaration of Independence.   Framed
       and glazed.
       One of the rare anastatic facsimiles.

1619   Facsimile of the autobiography of Abraham Lincoln.
       With fine portrait.   Published by James R. Osgood &
       Co., Boston, 1872.   Framed and glazed.

1620   Collection of Lincoln Medalets, circulated in 1860 and
       1864, and a Henry Clay medal, said to have been a
       pocket-piece of Abraham Lincoln.   17 pieces, in frame.

1621   Collection of Lincoln Campaign Medals of 1860 and 1864.
       11 pieces, in frame.

1622   Frame, containing notes issued by the Southern Confed-
       eracy during the war.

1623   Lincoln and Hamlin Presidential Election Tickets.   In
       English and German.   1860.   4 pieces.

1624   Collection of nine Lincoln Campaign Envelopes, and
       Lincoln and Johnson Presidential Election Ticket of
       Ohio.   In frame.

1625   Silk Badge, with Portrait of Lincoln.   Worn at Abraham
       Lincoln's funeral, 1865.   In frame.

www.ingramcontent.com/pod-product-compliance
Lightning Source LLC
Chambersburg PA
CBHW021113020726
47500CB00003B/735